Elvis Is Out There

Franz Douskey

Copyright © 2014 by Franz Douskey.

All rights reserved. Printed in the United States of America. No part of this book may be reproduced, or stored in a retrieval system, or transmitted in any form or by any means, electronic, mechanical, photocopying, recording, or otherwise, without express written permission of the publisher.

ISBN-13: 9781495423611
ISBN-10: 1495423611

About the cover photograph: Dewey Phillips worked for WHBQ and was the first deejay to play Elvis's records. In 1962, Dewey gave his buddy, T. L. Meade (Franz Douskey) a lot of papers and photos he was about to throw out. Among the photos given is the one used on the cover of this book.

Acknowledgments and Dedications

I've got to start with Sam C. Phillips, a most amazing man. Yes, he started Sun Records, first named The Memphis Recording Service: "We record anything, anytime." And that's where Sam recorded Howlin' Wolf, B. B. King, Jackie Brenston, Sleeping John Estes, Dr. Isaiah Ross, Rufus Thomas, Memphis Ma Rainey, Little Junior and Ike Turner. Sam was brilliant. He could sense talent. One of Sam's little known achievements is that he started the radio station WHER: all-women radio. The deejays, the technicians, the sales people—all of them were women. And this was in Memphis, in 1955. Sam brought in share-croppers, truck riders, cotton and poultry farmers, just a whole mess of people who would stand in front of an RCA double carbon microphone and change America's sense of music.

I've got to add Cowboy Jack Clement. Songwriter, engineer, talent hound. First to record Jerry Lee Lewis, wrote songs for Lewis and Johnny Cash, raised joyful hell, and when his Sun days were done he kept digging and brought Charley Pride front and center, carrying on Sam's work.

Scotty Moore kept Elvis going in the lean, early days as manager, driver and music inspiration. After the Colonel eased Scotty and Bill Black out of the Elvis scene, Scotty kept working, engineering, producing and playing. You can hear his licks as far back as Dale Hawkins' "Ain't That Lovin' You Baby," to the recent "706 ReUnion" with Carl Perkins.

I don't want to forget Dewey Phillips, no relation to Sam. Dewey worked at WHBQ and his show was called "Red, Hot and

Blue," a run of early Memphis music madness that eventually had national implications. Dewey played all kinds of music, and I do mean all kinds, which could have been a deep problem in the segregated south, but the music he played was stronger than Jim Crow impositions. Dewey radiated heat and energy, and kept himself fueled properly. By the early 1960s, Dewey had hit the skids, drinking a bit much but hoping to make a comeback. It didn't happen and Dewey was gone by 1968, at 43 years old.

Books have been written about Jerry Lee Lewis, Johnny Cash and Roy Orbison, so I won't spent much time writing about them here. One thing I do remember is that Johnny Cash told Roy Orbison to sing lower if he wanted to make it in music, and Jack Clement told Roy that he would never be able to sing a ballad. Even the great ones are wrong.

Not much has been written about Sam Phillips' older brother, Jud. Jud didn't know anything about recording or talent, but he did know how to promote Sun Records. He was the man who got Jerry Lee Lewis on the Steve Allen Show, Jerry's first national TV gig. Also, Jud made certain that the Sun record releases received radio time by paying off a number of deejays who worked for stations in the major market cities of New York, Philadelphia and Chicago. Usually, the disc jockeys were happy with cash, even a c-note would get air play for Carl Perkins, Johnny Cash, Billy Lee Riley, and Jerry Lee Lewis. Jud told me that there was a deejay in New York who would never take money. He insisted that Jud have appliances shipped to his home. Over the course of three years, Jud had sent no less than six refrigerators, several washers and dryers, four console televisions and two stoves. Jud never asked what the deejay did with all the appliances. Jud only cared about air time for Sun records. As long as Sun records were played on this deejay's radio and television shows, the appliances kept coming.

There was a brief alliance between Jud Phillips, Dick Clark and one of his sponsors, Beechnut Gum. Dick Clark was host of ABC's *American Bandstand*, a very popular afternoon music

Acknowledgments and Dedications

show with teenagers dancing to the hit records of the day. Dick Clark was so popular that ABC decided to add a prime time version of American Bandstand called *The Dick Clark Saturday Night Beechnut Show*.

The guests of the premiere *Beechnut Show* in February 1958 were Connie Francis and Jerry Lee Lewis. Connie had had a string of hits, including "Who's Sorry Now" and "Lipstick On Your Collar," and was rumored to be very close to Dick Clark. Connie sang first, then Jerry Lee Lewis came on to sing his brand new Sun record, "Breathless." Jerry Lee is singing and pounding away, but there is one problem. Because the song changes tempo at several intervals, the kids are having trouble dancing to "Breathless." To keep the sales of "Breathless" going, Jud thought up a promotion. Send two Beechnut gum wrappers and 50 cents, and you'll receive a copy of "Breathless" signed by Jerry Lee Lewis. Great. The gum wrappers arrive by the thousands, but there arose another problem. With Jerry Lee Lewis touring to promote "Breathless," how is he going to sign thousands of copies of the record?

This was no problem for Jud Phillips, the master of promotions. His first idea was to have rubber stamps with Jerry Lee Lewis' signature on them and stamp each record. But that required too much time, so Jud contacted the company that made the labels for Sun Records and had a facsimile of Jerry Lee Lewis' signature printed as part of the record label. Another success for Jud Phillips. The kids who bought the record either didn't notice or didn't care that the signature wasn't real.

Every now and then a copy of "Breathless" supposedly signed by Jerry Lee Lewis shows up on eBay.

There are a lot of stories about Sun Records. For example, Sam Phillips sold Sun Records to Shelby Singleton in 1963. This is still vivid for me because I was one of the interested parties competing against Shelby to buy Sun Records—including all its recordings and publishing holdings. Shelby was a very savvy producer. He hired Jimmy Ellis, an Elvis sound-alike, and released a 45 record of Ellis singing "That's All Right, Mama" (Elvis' first recording, in 1954, for Sam Phillips) on his new Sun Records label, in 1972.

In 1978, Shelby renamed Jimmy Ellis "Orion" and successfully marketed Orion's records. That lasted a few years, then Jimmy went back home and opened a package store. In 1998, Jimmy and his former wife were murdered at his store, Jimmy's Pawn & Package Store. The three robbers couldn't open the cash register, so they fled, only to be caught a few hours later.

Odd deaths weren't strangers to Sun musicians. Jerry Lee Lewis's two-year-old son, Steve Allen Lewis, drowned in the family swimming pool. Jerry Lee's 19-year-old-son, Jerry Lee Lewis drove into a bridge abutment and died on impact. Ray Smith—who had a few hits, including "Rocking Little Angel"—committed suicide when he was 45. Another label mate, Warren Smith, died at age 47 while preparing to tour Europe.

Roy Orbison wrote "Claudette," a song about his wife, Claudette Frady, that the Everly Brothers would record. Claudette was riding home one evening with Roy on separate motorcycles. Claudette slammed into a truck and was gone. In 1968, a fire broke out in Roy's Hendersonville home. The house burned to the ground and took the lives of his two older sons. Years later, Johnny Cash bought the Orbison land and put up an orchard where the house had been.

In 1956, Carl Perkins was riding high with the success of "Blue Suede Shoes," on his way to do the Perry Como Show, all the way north in New York. Their Chrysler rear-ended a truck. Carl suffered a broken collar bone and his brother Jay, who played rhythm guitar in the band, had a broken neck. That took care of the tour, and two years later Jay Perkins had died. It was at 706 Union one day, in 1962, when Carl came in to see Sam Phillips. Carl was broke, I'd say, desperate. He told Sam that he needed his royalty money right then and there. Sam owned Knox Music and HiLo Music, both publishers of Carl Perkins' music. Carl was edgy, gaunt, and when Sam told Carl that he didn't owe Carl

Acknowledgments and Dedications

any royalties, Carl really got hot. Some unchristian-like words were uttered, but Sam stayed cool. Sam floored even me when he asked Carl, "Do you remember that Cadillac I gave you?" And Carl nodded, yes. "Well, Carl," Sam said, "That was your royalties." I thought someone was sure going to die right in Sun Records. And to show you how stupid I was, I tried to intervene. "Carl," I said, "You ever think how many people would still be farming rocks in Arkansas and picking cotton if it weren't for Sam here? And I'm not only talking about black folk, but you guys, too." Carl just looked by me at Sam. Sam handed Carl some folded money and said he'd see what he could do. But I knew Sam and money seldom parted, so that pin money was just a way to ease the situation and get Carl on his way.

Pat Hare, one of the early blues artists and a heavy metal pioneer (according to Robert Palmer), recorded a song for Sun Records called, "I'm Gonna Murder My Baby." The song was prophetic because in 1963, while he was a member of Muddy Waters's band, Pat murdered his girlfriend and also shot a cop. In his last years in prison Pat Hare formed a band called Sounds Incarcerated. No recordings have surfaced.

Dr. Isaiah Ross, "The Harmonica Boss," recorded some great sides for Sun Records, including "Boogie Disease" and "Chicago Breakdown" He was one of the last one-man bands. The tragedy here is that he decided to quit music and took a job at the Ford Motor Company in Flint Michigan. I prize my video of him singing solo.

Many musicians went on from Sun Records to have notable recording careers. That list would include James Cotton, Rufus Thomas, Joe Hill Louis, Little Junior Parker, Little Milton, Sonny Burgess, Billy Lee Riley, Charlie Rich, Harold Jenkins (Conway Twitty), Bill Justis, Bill Black, Johnny Bragg (The Prisonaires, Confined To Tennessee State Prison), Ike Turner (with Tina), Walter Horton, Charlie Feathers, Jack Clement, and of course, Elvis Aron Presley, John R. Cash, Carl Lee Perkins, Roy Orbison, and Jerry Lee Lewis. Sun Records lasted about a decade under

Sam Phillips, but those were powerful years in a small recording studio where something new was happening every day.

This book is dedicated to Sam C. Phillips: the man who searched for "perfect imperfection" and found it. Thanks, Sam. Keep those sunglasses on.

Letter dated January 25, 1996

> "Dear Franz:
> …..You are a 'certified' fan and I personally greatly appreciate your knowledge and interest in my Life's Work. With gratitude, I am appreciatively,
>
> Sam C. Phillips"
> Founder of Sun Records and the man who discovered Elvis

Preface

Merle Haggard and I were sitting in a dumpy dressing room back stage at the Palomino Club back in 1981. The one in North Hollywood. He and I were talking about music and the subject of Elvis came up.

This was four years after Elvis had died, but Merle begged to differ. "You know, I was at the funeral. I was riding in the fourth white limosine. There was a viewing of Elvis before the funeral at Graceland. And I didn't want to go and look at the body, but it was just one of those things you gotta do. So I go up and when it's my turn to look into the coffin, I was really shocked. That's the way to describe it. I mean, there was a body in there, but to my dying day I'll swear that doesn't Elvis.

You ask Merle today, and he'll tell you the same story.

One: In The Beginning

Elvis had every reason to be proud. The United States Postal Service had just issued a commemorative stamp in his honor, an event marked by long lines and massive sales. Some post offices played Elvis music, while others hired Elvis impersonators. Other heroes had been honored by stamps, including Martin Luther King, Roberto Clemente, and John Kennedy, but Elvis was one up on all of them. They were dead when their stamps were issued, and Elvis was alive.

Elvis sat at the counter of a Dunkin Donuts along the Jersey Turnpike reading the New York *Times*. The article that had caught Elvis' eye was about Bill Clinton's Inaugural Parade. There was going to be an Elvis float in the parade, and on board would be several Elvis impersonators singing Elvis hits. It turns out that Bill Clinton is an Elvis fan. To prove it, he played his saxophone and sang Elvis songs on Arsenio and Imus. Forget that his sax sounded like a ruptured goose, and that his voice was gone; Bill Clinton, his voice ruined by the campaign, barely whispered "Don't Be Cruel" and "Teddy Bear".

Julie Gibson, the person in charge of the Clinton Inaugural Parade, has hired a number of people from Las Vegas who worked on Elvis's hair to find the best impersonators out of the more than three thousand applications received. To adhere to Bill Clinton's campaign pledge, the Elvis Inaugural float must reflect what America looks like. Out of the twenty Elvis impersonators on board, at least ten will have to be women, four African-American, three Latino, at least two will have to be homosexual, and a significant number will have to be single parents living below the poverty level. Zoe Baird, a long-time lobbyist for the rights of illegal aliens, and possible Attorney-General, has requested that her chauffeur, an illegal alien from Peru, who is like family, and earns thirty cents an hour above minimum wage, serve as driver for the float. It was hoped that some strings could be pulled before the parade so her chauffeur could get a driver's license, something that's not required in her home state of Connecticut.

Elvis ordered a refill and another powdered sugar jelly donut. Now that most people thought he was dead, he could go almost anywhere and enjoy reading about himself. He even toyed with the idea of going to the inauguration. he had gone to many events before where there were Elvis impersonators. He had even participated in Elvis look-alike and sing-alike contests. not only wasn't he discovered, but he never won. Too old, voice not strong enough. Elvis had lost fifty pounds and his voice had grown deeper and raspy, not like wheat being shot into a silo, but like a carload of coal rumbling down a galvanized metal air shaft.

At first, Elvis didn't like the idea of impersonators, then, while in a Trappist Monastery, he had time to think. They would carry on for him, help sell his records. He also knew that when he left the monastery, he would be able to move freely. If someone said he looked like Elvis, he could say he was an Elvis impersonator. After all, the A. A. E. I. (American Association of Elvis Impersonators) listed more than thirty thousand Elvis impersonators in their annual directory. More than twelve thousand showed up at their last convention.

Elvis finished his jelly donut and coffee, folded the *Times*, and paid the cashier, who tried not to stare. Elvis knew it was always the cashiers at donut shops and greasy spoon diners who recognized him the most, as though they were locked in on this invisible frequency. Some spoke up, but most didn't, either in awe or out of respect for his privacy.

Elvis climbed into his '89 Buick. He waved at the cashier who was still staring our the window. He drove off, thinking about the Inauguration and the Elvis float. It was all right, he thought. It's

One: In The Beginning

okay to have artificial Elvises at such a solemn occasion. After all, Bill Clinton was going to be the artificial president. Meanwhile, miles away in Phoenix, Jennifer Flowers was getting ready to host her daily talk show. Today's topic was Elvis. She had selected the music herself. The first number to come up was "I Forgot To Remember To Forget", followed by "I Was The One".

Two: Old Friends

Why did Elvis fake his death? Let him tell you in his own words. "Too many Moon Pies and Pepsis. That was it. People say I was hooked on uppers, downers, sidecars, and elevators and Dr. Nick. But I was really hooked on boredom. Like a caged animal, pacing back and forth, eating a dozen Moon Pies in an hour. The only way out was to fake my own death and take on a new identity."

Okay, you say, but whose body did they find on the bathroom floor in Graceland? I think it's safe enough to tell the whole truth now. The body they found belonged to Jimmy Hoffa. Some people don't know it, but Elvis and Jimmy were like this. They even had the same doctor, which is how Jimmy died.

I know you're going to say that Jimmy Hoffa didn't disappear until years later. But that was Hoffa's double that Jimmy kept with him to throw the Feds and any would-be assassins off his trail. When the union got word that Jimmy had died in Graceland, they moved in quickly to set the ringer up. Years later, when the ringer said he was going public about the real Jimmy, the mob rubbed him out and buried him in the endzone, between the goalposts, at Giant Stadium. So now you know why guy in the casket didn't look like Elvis.

The first thing that Elvis did was lose weight, grow a beard, and head for Boise, Idaho. He got a post office box under the name of Frank Floyd. Frank Floyd, as some of you know, was Harmonica Frank, who recorded for Sun Records around the same time Elvis cut "That's All Right". Elvis would always go

Two: Old Friends

to a relatively large city so he could get lost in the crowd. And who would look for him in Boise, Casper, Wyoming, or Peoria, Illinois?

He'd find a city he liked, check into a hotel, and stay on until he felt people had begun to recognize him. Every time he'd move to a new town, he'd get a new post office box under an assumed name. But there was always a pattern to the names. They were always the real names of musicians who had influenced him. He was Chester Burnett (Howlin' Wolf) in Bozeman, McKinley Morgenfield (Muddy Waters) in Salem, Riley King (B. B. King) in Bismarck, and Charles Berry (Chuck) in Pierre.

Only three people knew his whereabouts: Col. Tom Parker, Sam Phillips, and a woman know only as Annie Mae. He kept in touch with the Colonel so he could get money when he needed it. He kept in touch with Sam Phillips because it was Sam who had discovered him, cut his first records and served as an ally and mentor throughout Elvis' career. Not much is known about Annie Mae. You'll have to find out about her from other sources. It is fair to say at this point that Annie Mae was the most influential woman in Elvis' life after the death of his mother, Gladys. Everyone on the outside thought that Priscilla was the one, but no matter how the Colonel tried to keep Elvis away, it was always Annie Mae.

Elvis lived alone, travelling from city to city, until about 1987. Suddenly, he felt he could be himself and no one would recognize him. It worked in most cases, but there was the waitress in a Burger King, in Madison. She said she knew right away it was Elvis. He smiled, said that everyone knew Elvis was dead, and got out of town in a hurry.

Even through the beard, the gaunt face, and the ten years of living a hermitic life, Elvis forgot that he had something that could never be disguised or lost. Sam Phillips said it best at the mock funeral when he turned to Scotty Moore and said:

"Wasn't he something? I'll see him every time I close my eyes until the day I die. And then I'm not so sure I won't see him after that."

It's possible that when he closes his eyes he sees Elvis in that dinky twelve foot square studio on Union Avenue singing "That's All Right". Or maybe when Sam closes his eyes he sees all those hundred dollar bills floating down that could have been his but weren't because he sold Elvis to RCA for $35,000.

Needless to say, after the Madison Burger King incident, Elvis went into hiding again. This time in Coos Bay, under the name of Elias McDaniel, which would have pissed Bo Diddley to no end if he had known about it. Bo has this long story how Elvis used to go backstage at the Apollo and pick up Bo's moves. Could have happened. Bo was good. Not as slick as Jackie Wilson or as smooth as James Brown, but Bo could move. Only one problem with Bo's story. Let's look at those reprocessed 8mm reels of dizzy film taken in Memphis used car lots and high school gyms, and even a few hundred feet of silent, bleached frames of Elvis at some backwoods, say hallelujah, tent fair. He can't play the guitar to save his soul, but his hips have already slipped from neutral into overdrive, long before the Hillbilly Cat got to Fun City. So, later for you, Bo.

Does Elvis ever watch himself on tv? Nevah! Does he regret making movies. Yes. Every time Ted Turner has one of those Elvis retrospective weekends, Elvis not only wants to shoot the tv, but he'd love to go to Atlanta and shoot up TBS. But he feels Ted suffers enough, now that he's married to Jane. All that sweat, all that grunting while they STEP UP ($49.95) together, united in love, to Jane's latest video tape, "How To Think You Look Twenty-Five When Everyone Around You Knows You Look Fifty."

Elvis can remember when it only took seven bennies from his beloved physician to make him sweat like a hog in heat in two minutes. His advice to Jane? Check out that pre-nuptial agreement. Tell Ted to stop showing your movies over and over. The best one of yours is worse than the worst one of mine.

Two: Old Friends

Time for the first pop quiz. Who wrote "That's All Right"? Was it
- A. Elton John
- B. Paul Simon
- C. Bob Dylan
- D. Arthur "Big Boy" Crudup

Get this wrong and you are banned from reading the rest of this book.

Three: First Official Elvis Sighting

Just outside of Ohley, West Virginia, Merle Monroe was stabbed twenty-three times and his son, Glen, twelve times by a hitch-hiker Merle had picked up on his way to a laundromat. Monroe, and his three-year-old son, Glen, were left to bleed to death in a tomato field. Certain that he was going to die, Monroe scrawled the name of his assailant in the dirt. He then crawled more than a mile to his home to call police. He counted the number of peach trees he passed so he could tell the police where to find his son. Monroe suffered stab wounds to his chest, back, and a single gash that had gone through his right temple and into his brain.

Monroe doesn't remember anything after crawling across the ground, when he saw two black shoes directly in front of him. He was afraid it was the hitch-hiker who had come back to finish him off. He looked up, and it was Elvis. Merle remembers Elvis picking him up and carrying him before he blacked out. When he came to, he was in his house. Someone had called the police. One of the officers was holding three-year-old Glen, who had been stabbed in the chest and slashed across the throat.

Monroe's wife, Loretta, who was at work at a nearby poultry plant, had been called. Both Merle and his son were rushed to Wheeling General's emergency unit by helicopter. At the time, Monroe believed that his son had died. Dr. Louis Baker, director of the emergency unit, said, "This is a normal human being, but he had a tremendous will to live, to save his son."

Three: First Official Elvis Sighting

On Monday, when doctors told her that Glen would be all right, Loretta Monroe dressed him and took him to see his father for the first time since the stabbing. Monroe's eyes lit right up because he didn't think doctors were telling him the truth about his son still being alive. Baker said, "As soon as Monroe saw his son, he started getting better." It wasn't until a few days later that Monroe told about seeing someone who looked like Elvis.

Elvis responds. "I don't think I've been to West Virginia in thirty years. It's just that a lot of people look like me. Who else has impersonator conventions and witnesses who will testify that they saw me in two different states at the same time? And that Burger King-McDonald's thing is an exaggeration. I only go in there maybe once or twice a week. Hell, I'm no Bill Clinton. He's in there often enough to own a franchise."

Four: What Elvis Misses Most

Today the Post Master General announced that thousands of Elvis fans have been placing the elvis stamp on envelopes addressed to people who don't exist. That way the envelope is sent back stamped "RETURN TO SENDER." Collectors feel that this will make the stamps more valuable. The Post Master General said that if the trend kept up that he would have no alternative other than send all the envelopes to the Dead Letter Office. Several collectors have contacted the Post Master General, asking that he sell all envelopes affixed with the elvis stamps sent to the Dead Letter Office to them. They believe that envelopes stamped "Dead Letter Office" will be even more valuable than the ones stamped "Return To Sender." The Post Master General hasn't come out with an official statement on this, yet... As soon as he does, I'll pass it along.

    I asked Elvis if he enjoyed all the renewed attention he's received with the Elvis stamp and Bill Clinton tooting his songs on late night tv. Elvis said that he always hated crowds, that the last time he was really free was in 1956. He'd wake up and find people standing under the carport waiting to see him. But they were Memphis people. After signing with RCA, appearing on Milton Berle, Steve Allen, and Ed Sullivan shows, then starring in *Love Me Tender*, everything got out of control and he felt he could never walk down a streeet or ride a motorcycle alone again.

    What Elvis misses most now is Memphis, his mother, and a few friends. He'd love to sit down at a piano and sing spirituals all night. Maybe patch things up with Scotty Moore. Apologize to Jerry Lee Lewis.

I knew about the Scotty Moore thing. He was making a hundred dollars or so, and he asked Elvis for more money. This was after they had made a bunch of million sellers together. Elvis said, "No," although most folks knew it was the Colonel calling the shots.

Elvis said the worst things he ever did, other than appear on the Steve Allen Show wearing a tuxedo, singing "Hound Dog" to a Bassett, was playing practical jokes on Jerry Lee Lewis.

"I don't know why I did those things. The man had suffered enough, losing two sons, hiring a detective to follow one of his wives, only to have the detective and his wife fall in love and get married. I used to call him up in the middle of the night. I knew he'd be stoned, and most of the time I was, which is why I had to get away. I'd call up Jerry Lee and tell him I had to see him, to come over to Graceland. Meanwhile, I told my security people not to let anyone in. Jerry'd come driving up at 2 a.m., probably high on at least two or three things, telling the security guards to let him in 'cause I wanted to see him. Well, of course they wouldn't let him in. And Jerry Lee can get real mean. He was never that way, but the bad years of pain and frustration got to him. A lot of people let him down after it got known that he had married his 13 year-old cousin Myra, even before he had gotten divorce from one of his previous wives. The man was squirrelly. The press killed him and his good friend, Dick Clark, dumped him. Kept him off his tv shows and wouldn't play his records. After all Jerry Lee did for him.

Nobody would play Jerry Lee's stuff. Meantime, I got Priscilla living with me, she was just fifteen at the time, and I kept selling records. They went after Jerry Lee, not only ruining his career, but making him mean and bitter. There was no justice in it.

Anyway, I kept calling Jerry Lee late at night, maybe once every couple of months, and he'd show up. I'm sure Jerry hated me, because, let's face it, he had more talent. He could play more piano in a minute than anyone can play in an hour. I'd watch

Jerry on the closed-circuit security tv at the gate, explaining that I had called. One night he showed up with a gun and climbed to the top of the double gate in front of my place before the cops showed up. They arrested him, but I had the Colonel take care of things so there weren't any charges. And that was the last time I called Jerry Lee to come over. Later I learned that Jerry had accidentally shot his bass player in his dressing room. After that, I was really pulling for Jerry. I thought the movie about his life, *Great Balls of Fire,* might help him. That was a sorry movie. The guy who played Jerry acted like a clown. If they ever make a movie about my life, who are they gonna believe? Pricilla? Well, I've done my time in Hollywood, so I know what that's all about."

Elvis got quiet, looked up at the ceiling, then went over to the piano in his two-room apartment and began to play and sing "There Will Be Peace In The Valley" ever so quietly, as though he's afraid someone might hear him, call The National *Enquirer,* and Elvis would have to be on the move again.

Pop Quiz Number Two

Sam Phillips recorded Elvis, Johnny Cash, Carl Perkins, Jerry Lee Lewis, and Roy Orbison. How many are in the Rock & Roll Hall of Fame in Cleveland, Ohio?

    A. One
    B. Three
    C. Four
    D. Five

Five is the correct answer, but if you include Sam C. Phillips, the answer is six. Sam recorded Howlin' Wolf, Sleepy John Estes, B. B. King, Rufus Thomas, Junior Parker, Little Milton, Little Walter, Ike Turner, Roscoe Gordon, and Dr. Isaiah Ross, the Harmonica Boss, long before Elvis showed up at 706 Union Avenue to cut "My Happiness" as a birthday present for his mother.

Five: The Great Escape

A reader from Cincinnati has just faxed in wanting to know how Elvis escaped from Graceland. Did he leave before the funeral? How did they get Hoffa to look like Elvis? And how did they get Hoffa's body in the first place?

Let's take the last question first. Keep in mind that Elvis was always pro-law enforcement. If you get a chance, read Karl W. Daggett's scholarly study called *THE SECRET ELVIS*. Daggett correctly confirms that Elvis was a Federal Marshall appointed by Richard Nixon, that Elvis worked closely with the Drug Enforcement Agency, and even had agents play in his band and entourage as part of their cover. The Daggett book is difficult to find, because Colonel Tom Parker bought up all the copies. When the publisher decided to go into a second printing, the Colonel bought the publishing company. Daggett incorrectly concluded that Elvis was in danger from the mob and is now under the Witness Protection Program. Elvis considers the best books about him include Jerry Hopkins *ELVIS AND THE FINAL YEARS*, which touch on Elvis's government connections; Dave Marsh's *ELVIS*, and the essays by Greil Marcus in, Peter Guralnick's *LOST HIGHWAY* and . He hates the Albert Goldman book, considers it a piece of vengeance perpetrated by Memphis mafia turned mole, "Lardass" Fike, who hated Elvis because Elvis made him have surgery to lose some of his 350 pound girth.

To answer the second question, take a good look at Elvis in the coffin. It isn't Elvis. They did plastic sugery on Hoffa's face.

But look at the hairline. It's all wrong. And the nose. Elvis had a straight, Greek nose, not like the pug nose on the face in the coffin. Check out the jaw. Elvis had a full, heavy jaw. The one on the face in the box is sunken.

Everyone involved in the switch knew the face wasn't perfect, but they believed that the emotion of seeing what people thought was Elvis would carry the day. And for the most part it did. Those who were close to Elvis, but outside the circle of conspiracy, mentioned that he didn't look right. Merle Haggard said that he knew Elvis, and he know for certain that that wasn't Elvis in the casket. There was a lot of emotion. And you know how it is when someone great dies. People can't believe it. James Dean is supposed to be paralyzed, living outside of Dallas, Jim Morrison is alive in Paris, and Jimi Hendrix is living in the foothills, southeast of Tucson.

If you have any questions about whether that was Elvis lying in state, check with the Memphis medical authorities. All autopsy photos have gotten lost, the supposed contents of Elvis's stomach were flushed, all notes of the autopsy have become anti-matter and have disappeared. As a joke, Elvis wrote up the existing Death Certificate that's on file. You can write for a copy under the Freedom of Information Act, and make your own comparison. Elvis never thought that the certificate he wrote up would become the actual one on record, but at some point it was accidentally handed over to the authorities.

Now, back to the first question. How did Elvis escape from Graceland. Funny thing is that he never did. Elvis stayed there for months after August 16th. Graceland was closed to visitors, "for alterations," so the Colonel, a few close insiders, including Elvis's father Vernon, could figure out their next plan. There was plenty of money. Elvis's records started to sell again, and he soon became more valuable dead than alive. In any case, Elvis wanted out, and in a hurry.

Four months after the rigged funeral, Elvis had grown a beard and moved to Chattanooga, to Glen Island, to Tuxedo Junction,

Five The Great Escape

then to Kalamazoo to be with his long-time friend and confidant, Muhammad Ali. (I suggest you contact Ali on this. He will deny it, but he will smile.) That's where one of the early Burger King sightings occurred. After that, Elvis took off to Germany, travelling under the alias of John Burroughs. And that brings you up to date except for the sighting of Elvis on the steps of the Capital while Bill Clinton and Hillary walked through the streets after their inauguration. Was that Elvis? Yes. He had auditioned to be one of the Elvises on the Elvis Inaugural float but was rejected because he didn't look enough like Elvis.

Six: Out Of Body Travel

Barbara H. (name witheld by request) reports that an early RCA acetate given to her by Elvis talks to her. Barbara H. was very close to Elvis since their days together at Humes High School, in Memphis. The acetate was of "Anyway You Want Me", recorded on July 2, 1956, the day after Elvis appeared on the Steve allen Show in a tux. Barbara H. hadn't played the record in years, but felt like listening to it in November, 1977, a few months after the fake Elvis funeral, in August.

She always considered the acetate a treasure, and she has been offered $55,000. for it by a collector, in Boston, but now the record has taken on a new form. When Barbara H. plays it, she doesn't hear "Anyway You Want Me", but she does hear the voice of Elvis, distant, remote, telling her that he is alive and all right and for her not to worry. He'll reappear someday in Memphis and share a few laughs about high school with her. She says she can actually see Elvis as he is today: thin, bearded, wearing a burgundy flannel shirt and Levi's. Anyone else listening to the acetate hears the scratchy, muddied sound of Elvis singing.

It should be noted that Barbara H. isn't part of the TCB Inner Circle that knows Elvis is alive. She remembers going to the funeral, but she closed her eyes when she passed the casket because she was afraid to see Elvis dead. She wanted to remember him as the strange kid from Humes who called himself Valentino, wearing weird clothes white boys never wore and was forever being chased by short-haired punks who grew up hating anyone who was different.

Six: Out Of Body Travel

Her descriptions of Elvis bear little resemblance to the Elvis everyone remembers, but quite accurately describes the way Elvis looks today. She is even able to describe scenes and streets where Elvis has lived in recent years with uncanny accuracy.

As unique as Barbara H.'s experience is, it's not the only one that has surfaced. Troops in the Persian Gulf reported seeing Elvis's face in the clouds during a particularly intense battle. Within minutes, both the Iraqis and the United Nations forces stopped fighting and withdrew without orders from their military commanders. Some of the troops who were there have related the incident, and many were hospitalized for suspected battle fatigue syndrome.

A child was reported missing in Tulsa, in 1989. The parents, the police, neighbors, and the highway patrol searched for two days without finding the six-year-old child. During the second night after the child's disappearance, Elvis "visited" the parents' bedroom. The mother was the first awakened by Elvis's voice. She began to shake and sob uncontrollably as Elvis's face took form. At this point her husband woke up. They both witnessed this. Elvis told them that their daughter had fallen into a twenty-foot hole in an abandoned oil field a half mile from their home. He actually led them to the spot, and both parents crawled down on their hands and knees and called to their daughter, who answered them. When the parents looked up, Elvis was gone.

A crew from a nearby oil drilling company, local police and rescue teams were called to the site. It took more than eight hours to bring the six-year-old up from darkness to daylight. The girl was in fairly good condition considering that she hadn't had food or water for two days, and that she had suffered numerous insect and what appeared to be rodent bites. The father, who said he never cared much for Elvis, and never believed in visions or psychic experiences, tried to explain what happened, how Elvis had visited him and his wife and told them where his daughter was. The authorities said that he was under a great deal of emotional strain. When they pulled the little girl out of the twenty-foot hole, she was holding a little chain with a lightning bolt and TCB lettered in gold. The sheriff tried to take the chain for what he said was evidence, but he was told to take a hike because it was clear that the chain now belonged to the little girl who had been rescued by nothing more than a vision. Ask Elvis.

Elvis said that the night that the girl was rescued, he was in Houston to visit with Colonel Parker, who was 79, suffering heart problems and barely getting around on a wooden cane.

That same night, a trucker reported picking up a hitch-hiker on I-44. It was a chilly night, but the hitch-hiker wore neither a coat or a jacket. The trucker stopped at an all-night Stuckey's for coffee. His rider had fallen asleep. When he got back in his rig, not fifteen minutes later, the hitch-hiker was gone. The trucker reported that the hitch-hiker bore an uncanny resemblance to the young Elvis. He searched his rig for some evidence that Elvis was there. A coin, a signed photo, but there was nothing.

Seven: Bill Begins His Reign Of Error

Bill Clinton was sworn in yesterday. Tonight, Zoe Baird announced that she would withdraw her own nomination for Attorney General, because she had hired an undocumented alien to serve as her maid. In reality, Bill Clinton called her and told Zoe to drop out, because she was screwing up his administration before it even got started. I will not use the language attributed to President Clinton by my own personal mole, The Asp, but Bill suggested that he's never going to listen to Joe Lieberman or Chris Dodd again. He intimated that if the aforementioned gentlemen from the north proffer any advice in the future that he, Bill Clinton, would suggest, and I paraphrase here, that the two esteemed senators engage in the activity reserved for auto-necrophiliacs.

Instead, the President will now devote full attention to getting Congress to legislate a legal holiday honoring Elvis. Bill Clinton's brother, Roger, has donned a fright wig and is attempting to be to music what President Jimmy Carter's brother, Billy, was to beer. The President feels that Elvis has given more to Americans of his generation than, let's say, Abraham Lincoln, who strategised the defeated the South in the Civil War.

Here are President Clinton's priorities. Elvis Presley Day. He thinks he will be able to get the legislation through and allay any resistance by the Black Caucus as soon as he points out that it was Elvis who freed Little Richard, Fats Domino, Smiley Lewis, The Moonglows, and Maurice Williams, to name but a few, whose records were covered by Pat Boone, Gale Storm, The McGuire Sisters, and The Diamonds. Even now, Little Richard can't forgive what Pat Boone did to "Tutti Frutti". He swears that if he ever catches Pat Boone alone, he's going to punch out his lights and paint his white bucks black.

Next, President Clinton is going to allow homosexuals in the Army. I talked to Elvis about this on the phone one night.. He says he thinks only homosexuals should be in the Army.

President Clinton is going to institute his campaign promise of a middle income tax break. This is scheduled to go into effect the day after the Pope's wedding. President Clinton will work to pass the Illness/Family Leave Bill that will allow parents to take leave without pay to care for someone in their family. This week, the Commerce Department reports that 375,000 Americans took leave of their jobs. This used to be called being unemployed.

As far as the proposed Elvis Presley Day, Elvis is dead set against it. He is at that point where every minute is valuable. After all, as of this writing, he is fifty-seven. More fame isn't necessary. His records and other Presley Estate holdings brings in more than a billion dollars per year. And he usually gets by on less than a thousand dollars a month. Elvis feels that the only reason Clinton wants an Elvis Presley Day is so that he can embarrass himself again on alto sax on national tv.

Elvis remembers what fame was like, squeezing himself into those diamond studded jumpsuits and capes to play in front of an aging crowd in leisure suits and gray beehive hair do's. Everyone wanting the old songs while Elvis would rather sing "This Time, You Gave Me A Mountain" or "Don't Cry, Daddy." Songs that meant something to him right then. You know, living with a wife who was humping her karate instructor, while you're staying home eating Moonpies and drinking Pepsi's and trying to figure out where with all the fame, all the money, all that vibrant youth, where did everything go.

Talking on the phone longer than usual, Elvis says, "I'll tell you where everything went wrong. The very moment I signed on with the Colonel. Nice guy, but a hustler all the way. Out selling my photos for ten cents each while I was performing on stage.

Seven: Bill Begins His Reign Of Error

I even heard that back in the early eighties he had a life-size full-length photo of me and was charging ten dollars a head so people could have their pictures taken next to it. And this wasn't at some small town fair, but right in the lobby of the International Hotel, in Vegas. The Colonel. Did you know that he was born in Holland? Talk about Zoe Baird. To this day the Colonel is an illegal alien. The only difference between the Zoe Baird thing and me is that she told her aliens what to do, when to do it, and how high to jump, and with me, it was the illegal alien who told me what to do and when to do it.

"I still love him, but he was always out there making deals, only I'd find out about them later. And that gets me back to Bill Clinton. He reminds me of the early Colonel. Promise them anything, then go ahead and do what you want."

Then Elvis said he had to get off the phone, that we had been talking too long. He fears that someone will trace his calls and pinpoint where he is. I can tell you that he's somewhere in Virginia. I can tell you that now because by the time you read this, he won't be.

Eight: The Colonel And The Money

Mrs. Estelle Wobbleknobby, of Last Chance, Saskatchewan, writes to correct us about the Colonel and the Presley Estate. Mrs. Wobbleknobby accurately states that the Colonel was legaly cut off from the Presley Estate. However, in order to cut bait, the Presley Estate had to fork over more than $3.2 million in back royalties and up front money to cut off the Colonel's contracts with the Estate. Correction made.

For nearly twenty years, while serving as Elvis's manager, the Colonel took fifty per cent of everything. The Colonel was a frugal man. For example, whenever Elvis had a haircut, the Colonel would sweep up the clippings off the floor himself, for fear that a hired hand might miss a few strands. The Colonel would put the hair inplastic bags and sell them for $5.00 each at concerts. Elvis's haircut might cost a hundred dollars, but the Colonel would figure out a way to make a profit. Elvis says the Colonel has bank accounts under more than a dozen aliases. The Colonel had a reputation as a high roller at the Vegas tables. Some nights he has intentionally lost $25,000. and claimed that he had lost $75, 000 for tax purposes. With his established reputation as a compulsive gambler, a high roller prone to making terrible bets, the hotels that house the casinos welcomed him to stay, often for months on end, without charging him for his suite of rooms. The Colonel's theory was that the casinos will give better treatment to a known mark than they would someone coming from L.A. for a weekend. The Vegas mob thought they had the Colonel hooked, but in the end it was the Colonel who had suckered the mob, and walked away to tell about it.

A brief word about additional funds. Two months before the Elvis mock funeral, several life insurance policies, worth several million, were cashed in. Two checking accounts, containing $1,649,838.47 were closed. The insurance policies and checking accounts were in Elvis's name. This is all verifiable. According to best estimates, if Elvis were to spend $51,000 each day of his life, his accounts would increase by more than $4,200 per day.

Nine: The "B" Word: Another Sighting

The Helms family had lived in Harwinton, Connecticut, for eight generations in the same farm house along the Farmington River. But last summer things grew eerie. Three thousand bats suddenly took up residence in the walls of the old house. Robert and his wife Jessy began to hear squeaking and twittering sounds coming from behind their bedroom wall. Then they noticed bat droppings. Eventually, the bats would come into their bedroom at night, swarming so close to the Helms's faces that they could feel the vibration of wings.

Mr. Helms, a retired musician, is deathly afraid of bats, especially when more than 40 cases of rabid bats had been reported in the area that summer. He began to carry a tennis racket with him everywhere. He was so frightened of the flying rodents that they wouldn't allow anyone to use the "B" word.

Naturally, the Helms's called in several exterminators, but not one was successful in ridding the house of the nasty, drooling things. The Helms's called in local and state officials, but no one could get rid of the creatures. Ms. Helms called the The Department of Environmental Protection and they sent two experts who decided that the best way to get rid of the chiroteri was to fill the attic with moth balls. But that didn't work. Then they suggested Sonic devices designed to ward off rodents, which also didn't work.

An article in the Winsted *Citizen* about the bat infestation caught the eye of a former animal trainer, who studied bats as a hobby. Mr. Claude Fellow, a descendant of an ex-con named Danny Fisher,

Nine: The "B" Word: Another Sighting

who was a half-breed, who served in the Army, after he learned about civilized life from Ayn Rand who he claims was his social worker. Claude Fellow was shipped to Hawaii, where he became a fighter and owns a charter fishing boat that's been chartered to go to the World's Fair, in Seattle. But Claude can't go because he's supposed to be a lifeguard, in Acapulco, that summer, but on the way he gets lost, heads for Las Vegas and marries a woman who claims to be Ann Margret. After that he worked in a carnival, then a rodeo, before becoming a race car driver. Soon after, he teamed up with Sister Michelle working in a Chicago ghetto as a doctor. And Claude comes onto Sister Michell, only he doesn't know that Sister Michelle is a nun. He left Chicago and got a job with the Louisville Slugger company, in Kentucky. Anyway, Claude Fellow claims he knows something about bats.

He visits the Helms's and tells them that they have what amounts to a maternity colony. They can either wait until winter or they can hire an arsonist and burn the house down. Mr. Helms calls his insurance agent to double the coverage on his house, but his wife, Jessy, can't bear the thought of burning the bats. It seems she has looked at a few of the dead bats and noticed that each one bears a striking rememblance to Little Eddie and The Munsters is her all-time favorite tv show. Are these just bats, or are they miniature reincarnations of Little Eddie, even if Little Eddie isn't dead? She listened last night, and she thought she heard the bats squeaking in unison. It almost sounded as though they were singing "In The Ghetto".

The Helms's thank Mr. Fellow and decide to call in their minister, the Reverend Manson Petard. It is an unusual situation for him. Manson Petard is Presbyterian, and everyone knows the Roman Catholics have a contract with the Ecumenical Council that guarantees that all exorcisms go to them. But the Helms's have another plan. They ask their minister to read his sermon from last week on how we are all brothers and sisters and we should share with our less fortunate urban neighbors. Reverend Petard begins to read, raising his quavering voice to emphasize the injustices of the world and how we, with generous Christian spirit, should share with those less fortunate. Within ten minutes all the bats began to flee the house. The sky turned black with bats and the thrumming of wings was like the hum of a thousand threshing machines. Mr. Helms turned to his minister and said, "Thanks, Reverand Petard. If I'm awake during the collection next Sunday, I'll put a little something extra in the plate.

Ten: Lisa Marie At Twenty Five

This is the year that Lisa Marie turns twenty-five and takes complete control over Graceland and the Presley estate. It's difficult to imagine that so much time has passed, that the mantle has been placed in the hands of the next generation. Lisa Marie is married. It's impossible to imagine that Elvis is a grandfather.

Here are some of the plans developers have proposed for the dozen or so acres owed by the estate directly across from Graceland. 1. A mall with a small amusement park, called Presley Gardens. 2. Movie Complex called the Presley Cinema Art Complex. In this the developers promise that one theater will be devoted to the film works of Elvis, both commercial and documentaries shown constantly. Having viewed all the films, I'm not so sure whether this is a selling point or a threat.

Elvis agrees. He does like Charro (the movie, not to be confused with Xavier Cugat's 14th wife who has made a living by saying "Cucci, Cucci," on Hollywood Squares and other shows where they put famous people who have outlived their fame). Elvis also likes King Creole and thinks it has the best music of all of his movies. "The rest," he says, "they can burn."

POP QUIZ NUMBER THREE
From 1960 through 1969, how many movies did Elvis make?
    A. Four
    B. Seven
    C. Eleven
    D. Twenty-seven

The film that made the most money was Blue Hawaii; the one that made the least was Charro. His four best-selling songs from his movies were also the titles of the movies: "Loving You", "Jailhouse Rock", "Blue Hawaii", and you tell me what the fourth one is.

Along the same line of thought, Elvis, at one time, thought "Jailhouse Rock" was the worst song he ever recorded. He now thinks that "Do The Clam", "Bossa Nova Baby", "Surrender", or possibly "Wooden Heart" are. He also regrets changing the line from "One Night". The original goes, "One night of sin is what I'm now paying for." Elvis was encouraged to change it to "One night with you is now what I'm praying for." This is similar to Mick Jagger, so anxious to continue national exposure on American tv, who changed "Let's Spend the Night Together," to "Let's Spend Some Time Together," to please Ed Sullivan, the man who decided to save America from depravity by shooting Elvis from the waist up.

The answer to Pop Quiz Number Three is D, Twenty-seven. How many of them netted more that $5,000,000? All of them. "Love Me Tender" was a hit single from the movie of the same name. Or as Elvis calls it, "The beginning of the Hollywood specialists, cutting up my music and leaving it still beating on the floor. They gave me the Ken Darby Singers and I kept looking around for Scotty and Bill. I should of quit right there, but they were throwing this money. And I thought it was worth something?"

Eleven: Elvis & The Conspiracies

One of the explanations for Elvis's desire to escape from Graceland has been that he knew too much about the Robert Kennedy and Martin Luther King assassinations. It has been explained that Elvis is a Federal Marshall, appointed by Richard M. Nixon. Elvis's fascination with guns and self-defense are well-documented, as are his relationships with the Los Angeles and Memphis Police Departments, the sites of the Kennedy and King murders.

Everyone in the world, except those who served on the Warren Commission, knows that Lee Harvey Oswald didn't act alone. Elvis says he knows Hoffa was involved and was in partnership with the C.I.A. for two reasons. As Attorney General, Bobby Kennedy was determined to throw Jimmy Hoffa out of the Teamsters and into jail. Meantime, Jack Kennedy was determined to disband the C.I.A. because, even though it cost the government upwards of $3,000,000,000 a year, the C.I.A. never once accurately predicted a coup, a war, or a change of power. Instead, they spent time and money burning cane fields in Cuba, assassinating leaders in South East Asia, and propping of unpopular governments that were corrupt from within.

This is how Elvis sees the structure of American government. Most powerful is the C.I.A., then comes the multi-nationals like Exxon and A.T.&T., that once offered Chilean military leaders a million dollars to overthrow the government of Savador Allende. After the multi-national, comes the Pentagon, then the 80,000 lobbyists to pay off senators and representatives, then comes the Office of the President. Maybe the F.B.I comes before the presidency.

Because of this friendship with the Los Angeles Police Department, Elvis knows that Sirhan Sirhan didn't act alone. There is even evidence that the gun fired by Sirhan was not the same caliber of the bullets that killed Robert Kennedy. And there is no way that James Earl Ray acted alone. He was a petty thief. How did he end up in Europe with fifty thousand dollars? Why was the fire station across from the Lorraine Motel put on a skeleton crew the day of the assassination? Where were the police who were assigned to guard King? Why was Bobby Kennedy led through the kitchen of the hotel? Why was John Kennedy's motorcade route changed? Elvis says that the changes were made by the C.I.A. and by the mob connections, including Sam Giancona, the C.I.A. proposed to Robert Kennedy to assassinate Fidel Castro.

I ask Elvis if he's under a Federal Protection Program. He laughs and says that if he was under a Federal Protection Program, it would be like having the fox guarding the hen house. It's best if only a few people know where he is, what he looks like, and what his name is this week.

Elvis goes through about two or three names a month. Recently he has been Richard Tracy, William Charles Fields, John Armstrong, and Robert Wills. And where is he happiest? In Europe, in the woods, fishing in Montana, or any place where there is a lot of sky. And what about Memphis? No, he says, it's too crazy now, and they'd recognize him in a minute. Besides, most everyone he loved there is gone, dead, except a few. He'll go back one day. But not now. Too many scars, he says. Elvis talking about scars? I tell him he could go anywhere and no one will recognize him.

Twelve: The Million Dollar Trio

Elvis considers 1956 as the greatest year of his life. His records were selling well, he could still walk down the street without people stampeding him, and everyone he loved was still alive. Oddly enough, Elvis considers his greatest moment in music was the afternoon of December 4, 1956, when he decided to stop by the old Sun studios on Union Avenue. Carl Lee Perkins was cutting "Matchbox" and "Your True Love". He was using a kid from Ferriday, Louisiana, on piano. Back then, Jerry Lee Lewis was earning $10.00 as a session pianist. This was before he cut "Whole Lotta Shakin' Goin' On", which Jerry Lee will tell you sold more than eighty million records, and that Sam Phillips still owes him four million dollars in royalties.

Johnny Cash was at the studio at the time, but he ducked out to do grocery shopping after joining in on "Almost Lost My Mind", "Blueberry Hill", and a few Mary Robbins songs.

"That was a great afternoon, no pressure, just to sing for pleasure," Elvis says. He points out that most of the songs that Jerry Lee, Carl, and he did together were spirituals, because that was the common thread through their lives. All three men were born poor. Elvis grew up in a shotgun house, in Tupelo, Mississippi, that was built by his father, Vernon, for about $150. It was called a shotgun house because it was so long and narrow and no rooms in between that you could fire a shotgun through the front door and never hit anything between the front door and the back door. Funny thing is that the $150 house is an official registered Historic Site in the State of Mississippi.

Carl Perkins was born on a tenant farm outside of Tiptonville, Tennessee. Wrote most of his own material, and claims that Sam Phillips owes him millions of dollars in back royalties. Jerry Lee Lewis grew up poor in Ferriday. The way he tells it, he had the natural God-given talent right from day one, and very few would dispute it. He says he took up piano at age eight, then he got really good when he broke his leg and sat at the piano for six weeks straight, his right leg sticking out, which is how he developed his style.

But all three had a serious religious upbringing. As Elvis says, "When you're poor, all you can do is hope for a better world." Even though the three men came from different states, they grew up learning the same songs: "Take My Hand, Precious Lord"; "There'll Be Peace In The Valley"; both written by Thomas A. Dorsey, a former blues-musician who got religion. Thomas A. Dorsey died last week, at the age of 93. They said he had Alzheimer's, but some people said he had gone onto the other side and was having visions during the last few years of his life. One time, in a moment of lucidity he was asked to try and focus on this world. He is reported to have said: "Child, I have seen enough of this world," and he never again made any sense to the people who didn't understand that he was having visions of the Beautiful City.

That autumn afternoon and night at Sun Studios Elvis sang some of his hit songs, too. When he sang "Don't Be Cruel", he talked about a young singer with Billy Ward & The Dominoes. At the time, Elvis didn't know that the young singer was none other than Jackie Wilson, who later had a bunch of hits, including "Lonely Teardrops", "I'll Be Satisfied", and "Talk That Talk".

At the time, Billy Ward was playing in Las Vegas. So was Elvis. And it was a painful experience. Elvis says he really bombed. Too many old people. They just looked at him, stared, while he sang "Tutti Frutti". They should have booked Lawrence Welk. It took Elvis nearly fifteen years before he felt confident enough to go back to Vegas. When he did, he broke every attendance record

Twelve: The Million Dollar Trio

in the whole town. They even put up a statue of him in the lobby of what was then The International.

Elvis says that the session at the old Sun studio was one of the last times that music was fun. There was something powerful and spiritual about the old studio. How else can you explain that Howlin' Wolf, B. B. King, Roy Orbison, Johnny Cash, Jerry Lee, Conway Twitty, Sleepy John Estes, James Cotton, Dr. Ross, Junior Parker, Sonny Burgess, Rufus Thomas, and Billy Lee Riley all end up at 706 Union Avenue? There has got to be a divine force there. People head off to Arizona, New Mexico, Tibet, or Peru to find spiritual centers in the world. Try 706 Union Avenue, back in time.

Elvis remembers walking out of the studio that December night. It was dark and getting chilly. He remembers it as a Saturday afternoon. I do some backtracking and find out it was on a Tuesday, which makes sense. If it was Saturday, everyone would have been on the road.

"I remember walking out of there that night. I felt so good inside that studio. I felt safe. It was like every good feeling I'd ever had, had gathered in me. I had returned to my home, Sam Phillips had always been good to me, my mom was still alive, and I was a millionaire. I mean, right at that moment I had it all. And as I started to leave the studio, some overpowering dread came over me. I felt it in my knees. I began to feel a little sick. As soon as the studio door opened on the night, a cold wind blew in. We had been in the studio for so long, I was surprised to see it dark outside. I'll tell you this now, because I didn't know it then. From the minute I walked out of the studio until right this minute, I have never stopped being scared. I was scared every time I had to record. I was scared every time I had to go out on stage. I tried everything not to be scared. Tranquilizers. Meditation. Nothing worked. And I think I was always scared. Take a look at the first picture anyone ever took of me. Wearing a floppy hat tilted over my right eye. I remember the moment. I was scared. And maybe I was scared before that. You know, some kind of memory of birth.

You know, when my brother Jesse died. It's only by some weird fluke that I'm here and he And how about this. Maybe I'm really Aron, and it was my twin brother, Elvis, who was stillborn. and all along I'm a case of mistaken identity, the world's first Elvis impersonator. No, man. I remember everything. And that night in the studio. That wasn't thirty five years ago. That was last night."

Elvis looks up at me, as though he's suddenly remembered I'm in the room. He looks at the tape-recorder on the table.

"You recording this?'

I nod, yes.

"Well, you got to warn me. Now turn that damn thing off."

Thirteen: Elvis Has Left The Building

POP QUIZ NUMBER FOUR
What was the name of the hair rinse company and the color dye Elvis used? Sorry, this one is not multiple choice. You either know your stuff or you don't.

What was the name of the guitar player used by Elvis during his last concerts and recording sessions? He also played lead on Dale Hawkins "Suzie Q" and on most of Ricky Nelson's Imperial sides.
    A. Eric Clapton
    B. Carlos Santana
    C. Eric Burton
    D. Jerry Garcia
    E. Hank Garland
    F. James Burton
    G. Chet Atkins
    H. Richard Burton

During the late sixties Elvis happened to be particularly fascinated by one tv show, The Prisoner. It was during the summers of 1968 and '69, on CBS. Elvis identified with the lead character, The Prisoner, also known as Number 6, played by Patrick McGoohan. Elvis saw himself as a prisoner, Number 8 (eighth degree black belt), who, like McGoohan, could not escape. Was he a prisoner or was he being tested? Who could he trust and who were the spies? who were the people who would help him and who were the hangers on who would gradually drag him down?

McGoohan finally escapes by outwitting those around him who pretend to be his allies. So it was back in the summers of '68 and '69 that the seeds for escape were planted in Elvis's mind. The plan would take awhile to put into effect. There were a number of people depending on him for their livelihood, and he genuinely cared about them.

Over the years he would give the musicians and his backup vocal groups more of a percentage of his income and give them exposure so they could eventually make it on their own. As soon as he felt everything was in place, he made his move. It was painful, and life might be lonely. But Elvis always said that the bigger the auditorium, the larger the crowd, the more insolated and lonely he felt. There were dozens of times he wanted to climb off the stage and get closer to the crowds. He wanted to stop and talk to people on the street, at the airports, but that was impossible. He was surrounded by bodyguards and security that by their mere presence kept not only the crowds, but Elvis as well, at a distance.

As Elvis left Graceland weeks after the funeral; He left Memphis in a plane purchased from Jerry Lee Lewis. Elvis yelled from the runway, "Elvis has left the building," meaning Graceland, a building that in many ways had become a living mausoleum, with too many memories of happier times. He had to leave or eventually be consumed by the confines of stardom. And youth had long left him, and yet he was expected to still be the Elvis of old, happy to sing the old songs for the fanswho were clinging to the wrong illusions and false memories. Elvis had left that building many years ago.

Back to the pop quiz. What color dye did Elvis use. There are two schools of thought. Some report that Revlon made a special formula for Elvis called Blue Velvet. You can notice the shinny blue tinge to his hair in his movies. The other school insists that it was Clairol Black Velvet.

Right now Elvis' hair is dark brown with gray at the temples and interspersed with the brown throughout. He generally combs his hair once or twice a day and that's it.

Pop Quiz question two. The answer is James Burton, the premier rock guitar player of all time, who not only should be enshrined in the Rock n Roll Hall of Fame, in Cleveland, but probably deserves a postage stamp of his own.

Fourteen: The Little Footsteps In The Snow

Elvis would like everyone to know that he is not responsible for most of the numerous sightings reported in the various newspapers throughout the world, especially those that link him to miracles and visions. Just this morning a four-year-old girl was released from a Syracuse, New York hospital after recovering from exposure. It was just last week that Alicia Cartwright was found in a snowdrift. The EMT's pronounced her dead at the scene. One doctor actually credited the cold and immediate cardiopulmonary revival for her survival. Alicia's mother, Louise Cartwright, said, "I think it was Elvis who saved her," at a hospital news conference.

Alicia, wearing only her Dr. Denton's, was found blue and rigid in 16 degree weather, at least three hours after she wandered out of her home to look for her lost dog, named Buttons. Alicia's physician, Dr. Miriam Borge, said that Alicia's recovery, "is highly unusual. There is no evidence of brain damage, and there is some slight tissue damage from frost bite in her left little toe. But other than that, she is a miracle child."

Evidently, Alicia wandered out into the night while her parents were asleep. Her dog, Buttons, had disappeared earlier in the day. Mrs. Cartwright said she had a dream about Colorado. She was skiing, when suddenly there was an avalanche of snow. Unable to breathe, Mrs. Cartwright woke up shaking and perspiring. She was filled with fear because the dream was so real. Then, as she sat up, she saw Elvis's face in her bedroom window. He was saying something and pointing

Fourteen: The Little Footsteps In The Snow

outside, toward the backyard. Then she heard him say, "she's outside, in the snow."

At that point, Mrs. Cartwright ran into her daughter's room and found that Alicia wasn't in her bed. Mrs. Cartwright screamed, which woke up her husband, Jeffrey. Mrs. Cartwright ran through the kitchen and out the back door. Her husband followed. Mrs. Cartwright said she felt as though she was being controlled by a force or power that led her directly to the snowbank where Alicia had fallen unconscious.

Mr. Cartwright, a Syracuse policeman, immediately applied CPR until the medical team arrived. Even though Alicia Cartwright was pronounced dead at the scene, through some miscommunication, or in Mrs. Cartwright's words, "divide intervention," Alicia was rushed to the Mercy Center Hospital, in downtown Syracuse. When Alicia reached the hospital, Alicia's body temperature was 72 degrees. Her heart had stopped beating. Medical personnel tried various resuscitation techniques for more than four hours before Alicia's heart resumed beating.

The family dog, Buttons, was recovered from the Syracuse dog pound where it had been taken because a neighbor had complained that the dog was allowed to run around loose in violation of the city's Leash Law.

It is interesting to read the various stories about Elvis appearing in moments of crisis in the local papers, and even in the super market tabloids. So many incidents have occurred, that the author of the book LIFE AFTER LIFE has come out with a book about the various psychic and physical experiences people have had involving Elvis. The book is called THE PSYCHIC ELVIS or LIFE AFTER ELVIS. Something like that. I haven't read a copy and Elvis won't let it in the cabin where we're staying for a few weeks, situated just north of J.D. Salinger's house, in Cornish, New Hampshire.

I go out from time to time, just to get some air and see people. Elvis, on the other hand, seldom leaves the cabin or the apartment, depending on where we're staying,, especially during the day. Right now he's reading Lao Tzu and has no interest in being a part of other people's psychic phenomenon. After all these years trying to become invisible, it seems that there are more Elvis sightings now than when he was young and so desparate to be noticed. Isn't that exactly how it is, as though the Gods hear everything we tell them in reverse.

Fifteen: The Art of Invisibility

This morning Elvis and I went out ot breakfast at a small place called The Memory Restaurant. We took a booth in the back. I ordered pancakes and sausage. Elvis ordered two scrambled eggs, whole wheat toast, dry, and a side order of home fries. We talked briefly about the article in yesterday's paper about the girl, Alicia Cartwright, found in the snow bank, in Syracuse. How exactly is she going to explain to her friends that she was saved by Elvis. Her friends will ask, "What's an Elvis?"

Elvis says that as a kid he wanted more than anything else to be invisible. To be able to walk in a crowd unnoticed. To walk through walls. "And," I said, "to visit the girls' shower room at Humes High." Elvis laughed. "Yeah, that would have been all right, too."

Elvis said he remembered an old radio show from his childhood. Everyone thinks that all Elvis listened to was The Grand Ole Opry and a few blues stations, but his favorite radio show was The Shadow. Elvis remembers that the show used to come on around five o'clock, Sunday afternoons. He used to like to listen to it in the winter when it would be dark by five. He'd lie on his bed next to the small Crosley radio. The theme music would come on ("Omphale's Spinning Wheel," Opus 31, by Saint Saens), followed by the announcer, Andre Baruch saying, "Once again, your neighborhood Blue Coal dealer brings you the thrilling adventures of The Shadow, the hard and relentless fight of one man against the forces of evil. The Shadow, mysterious character who aids the forces of law and order, is in reality Lamont Cranston, wealthy young man-about-town. Several years ago in the Orient, Cranston learned a strange and mysterious secret, the hypnotic power to cloud men's minds so they cannot see him. Cranston's friend and companion, the lovely Margo Lane, is the only person who knows to whom the voice of the invisible Shadow belongs." The show would end with The Shadow saying, "The weed of crime bears bitter fruit. Crime does not pay. The Shadow knows." Then he would laugh his famous, eerie, all-knowing laugh."*

That was Elvis's dream then, and it's the same now. How to be invisible. And like Cranston, Elvis is studying the writings from the mysterious East. Elvis has considered other methods of gaining partial invisibility. At one point plastic surgery was given some thought. Even though Elvis's features have changed over the years, he wanted to alter his facial features so that vestages of the old Elvis didn't exist. He wanted to change the classic line of his nose to a flatter, Eastern European shnozz. Narrow his eyes. Wear brown contacts. Grow a beard, which he eventually did. But at this point in Elvis's life, he actually likes it when someone recognizes him. Sometimes they know but try not to react, because they know it can't be him because he's supposed to be dead. Others clearly recognize him, know who he is, but out of respect and understanding, they nod and move on. The most difficult group to handle are those people, mostly women, who recognize him and can't control themselves. They scream, and some run up to Elvis to touch him or hug him.

Of course, Elvis denies that he's Elvis most of the time, especially to the screamers. It is with this group he wishes he had the power of invisibility. However, on a rare occasion, a woman will come up to him quietly and say, "I know you're Elvis," "I know who you are," or even "I love you," and walk away.

It is because of women who acknowledge him quietly that Elvis decided not to alter his features, because even Elvis needs someone to come up to him from time to time and tell him that she loves him. Maybe I shouldn't say, "even Elvis," I should say, "especially Elvis," needs signs of life and words of love, no matter how fleeting.

Fifteen: The Art of Invisibility

Men, on the other hand, are weird. They sometimes recognize Elvis, but they seldom acknowledge him. Something's wrong. Either they can't or won't reveal their sense of surprise, and/or are afraid they might be wrong. After all, men are such logical creatures. How can this be Elvis when everyone with any sense of logic knows that Elvis is gone?

But Elvis still likes the idea of becoming invisible. Imagine being able to travel anywhere without waiting in line or paying for an airline ticket. Imagine sitting invisibly in the White House and listening to Hillary tell Bill what to do, because let's face it, since the Jennifer Flowers thing, Bill Clinton, even though he's president, in Hillary's eyes he is a dead man. Imagine sitting next to Jane Fonda and Ted Turner while they wave their rubber tomahawks to cheer the Atlanta Braves on to another World Series humiliation. Imagine being able to see what Ann-Margret looks like after all these years.

"Ah, yes," Elvis sighs. Then he rethinks himself and decides it's better to remember Ann-Margret as she was when they were both in Viva Las Vegas. She had the greatest legs, the strongest legs, and so long, they seemed to go on forever.

Elvis sips his coffee and sits back. Yeah, he says, he'd like to have the power to become invisible, but as far as Ann-Margret goes, he'd rather have a time machine and go back with what he now knows. He laughs quietly, so as not to create any attention. We laugh because we both know there is only one time machine and it's locked in forward and seems to be going much faster than it ever did before.

*The Shadow is a copyrighted feature of Conde-Nast publications

Sixteen: Revisions and Updates

A few chapters back I mentioned a book that deals with various psychic experiences. Lillian Whitmore, of Elmira, New York, has written that the correct title is ELVIS AFTER LIFE, written by Raymond A. Moody, Jr., M.D.

Another woman, Barbara Highsmith, writes that she likes the pop quizzes in the book and wonders if it would be possible to devote an entire chapter to test her knowledge. Dear Barbara, the questions for the pop quizzes usually come up as part of the writing. I haven't thought about putting a chapter together solely of questions about Elvis. But enough people have said that the quizzes are their favorite part of the book that perhaps not only will we have more pop quizzes, but maybe a midterm and a final exam, as well.

The latest update on the Elvis stamp follows. Some collectors have put four stamps in plexiglass baseball card holders and are selling them at $5.95 each. The Post Office has made so much money that they will be putting out another series of stamps devoted to Rock n Roll this summer. Among the stars to be included are Bill Haley, of Bill Haley and the Comets, famous for "Rock Around the Clock", "See You Later, Alligator", "Shake, Rattle and Roll", stolen from Big Joe Turner, and "Dim, Dim the Lights".

Buddy Holly is another definite candidate for a stamp, if you can stand that nasal, girlish-man voice. Sam Cooke could be a choice, but the spector of him being gunned down in a motel by the owner who claimed that Sam was assaulting Elisa Boyer might eliminate him.

Of course, one of the requirements is that you've got to be dead, or at least thought to be dead. That opens the door to J. P. Richardson and Richie Valens, who died with Buddy Holly in a plane crash. This reminds me of a story Waylon Jennings told me He was working with Buddy Holly as one of the Crickets, Buddy's backup group, playing electric bass. Waylon was scheduled to fly with Holly, but at the last minute he gave up his seat to Valens, who had a bad cold. The Holly-Valens-Big Bopper plane ices up and crahses right after take off. Nobody survives, not even the pilot About three years ago, Waylon ws in Phoenix and he had a reservation to fly to Dallas-Fort Worth. But something spooks Waylon. While passengers are boarding the plane, he goes to the bar, raises a few and takes a later plane. Damn, if the plane Waylon was scheduled to fly on doesn't crash, killing seventeen people. So, if you're ever on a plane with Waylon and you see him get up and get off, my suggestion is that you do the same.

Ricky Nelson is another possibility for a stamp this summer. Ricky died in a plane previously owned by Jerry Lee Lewis. The same plane Elvis flew out of Memphis in when he left Graceland. Never, and I mean never, buy a used airplane from Jerry Lee Lewis.

How about a stamp for Dee Clark, who sang "Hey Little Girl" and "Raindrops", who died last year in Atlanta, where he was a janitor in a welfare hotel. How about a stamp for Blind Lemon Jefferson who wote "See That My Grave Is Kept Clean", but is buried in an unmarked grave in a field, isomewhere in Texas. Maybe Jackie Wilson deserves a stamp. He sang "Lonely Teardrops", "Talk That Talk", "Doggin' Around", and he could outmove James Brown, but suffered a stroke while performing stage in a Dick Clark revue. Jackie Wilson lay in a coma for years, and never recovered. As he sang once, "There is no pity in the naked city."

Let's have a stamp for Johnny Ace, who shot himself back stage in Houston, on Christmas Eve, in 1954, while his single for Duke Records, "Pledging My Love", became a million seller.

Maybe we could get a large, oversized stamp featuring Joplin, Hendrix, Morrison, and other rock stars who have overdosed themselves into the great oblivion netherland.

Elvis's choices for stamps are as follows. Hank Williams, dead at 29, wrote more than 1,200 songs, including "Your Cheatin' Heart", "Honky Tonk Blues", and "You Win Again". Jimmie Rodgers, the Singing Brakeman, has already had a stamp, but Elvis thinks he deserves another. When Jimmie Rodgers was dying of TB, he came up to New Jersey to cut his last songs. He'd do a take, then he had to lie down for an hour or so before he had the strength to cut another song.

Another Elvis choice is Patsy Cline, in his mind the best straight out country singer of his generation. Also, let's not forget Chicago. Howlin' Wolf, Muddy Waters, Sonny Boy Williamson, Little Walter, all finishing up at Chess Records, where people like Mick Jagger, John Lennon, Bob Dylan and Bruce borrowed, imitated, and were influenced by their music.

Meanwhile, the United States Postal Service has announced that Elvis has sold more than seven million stamps to date. They have sold so many stamps that the Post Master General has announced that the Postal Service will not need a rate increase this year. Phase two will include a book about Elvis, special date of issue stamps postmarked from Graceland ($5.95 each), and a 12' x 12' poster of the stamp for $14.95. In fact, if business gets any better, the United States Postal Department will get out of the mail business and open up another souvenir shop across from Graceland, on what used to be called Highway 51, but is now called Elvis Presley Boulevard.

Seventeen: Graceland

During his last days at Graceland, Elvis says he didn't eat regular meals, he grazed. He'd eat almost all the time while watching television. He had grown as sedentary as a slug. Now he seldom eats more than twice a day. On Wednesdays and Sundays he eats only one meal. His usual routine is to eat a hearty breakfast. He has cut back on well-cooked (burned) bacon, but still likes fried eggs at least three times a week. He might have a small lunch, but usually he skips it, and has a simple dinner. Last night he had stir-fried vegetables with brown rice covered with tamari sauce. He says he feels better and it helps him keep his weight down. When Elvis left Graceland he had a 44 inch waist. It's now down to a mean, lean thirty-two inches.

Occasionally, Elvis will binge. He still loves the taste of a super well-done, beyond repair hamburgers. If he stays up late, he has a tendency to eat more than he'd like to, as though the food goes in unconsciously. Because of this, Elvis has insisted that after eight o'clock the refrigerator is off-limits.

The worst times for Elvis are when he's worried or nervous. If he thinks he's been spotted and will have to move as a result, he gets upset and eats more than he should. Elvis feels that his childhood has a lot to do with his terrible eating habits. With the poverty, and with Elvis's father Vernon being chased and arrestedby the police for stealing a pig or for writing bad checks, there was a lot of insecurity in the Presley household. They moved from the shotgun house in cozy Tupelo, to subsidized housing in sprawling Memphis in 1951. Often, there was a question where the next meal would come from. It's difficult to imagine Elvis and that level of poverty. Remember, Elvis grew up in a house without electricity until he was eight or ten, old enough to begin listening to the radio which helped him forget the day-to-day battle over food, warmth and whether his father would get home or spend time in jail.

Elvis fans will blanch at the thought of Elvis eating brown rice in tamari sauce. He also uses chop sticks. But he won't apologize. He says those double burnt hamburgers were great, but some good times must come to an end or else everything will come to an end. He finds that using chop sticks slows him down. Meals are something to anticipate and savor. He used to eat four hamburgers and never taste one. Food was just something to fill the emptiness inside that wasn't hunger, that was anxiety, that wasn't anxiety, but was fear. And what were some of the fears? He was gaining weight and that made him anxious. Food had a calming effect for awhile. So, the cycle began. Everytime he felt upset, he would head for the refrigerator.

Much of Elvis's life got out of hand after the Pricilla situation, which Elvis will not discuss. Another thing that caused him anxiety was the costuming which the Colonel insisted he wear. And when it came to the Colonel, Elvis always caved in, even when it was against his better judgment, because he felt he owed the Colonel everything. But he should have never let The Colonel give Scotty Moore, Bill Black and J.D. Fontana the runaround. While Elvis and The Colonel were making millions, Scotty, Bill and D.J. were getting a hundred dollars a week. And they were *the* sound behind Elvis. That was the problem. The Colonel wanted to change Elvis's music, clean it up, make it smoother, accessible to a wider white audience. He couldn't do that with Scotty, Bill and D. J. around. So, The Colonel kept them broke. And he kept Elvis out of the picture. Elvis wasn't going to continue to be The Hillbilly Cat if The Colonel had anything to say about it, and as it turned out, he had everything to say about everything.

Seventeen: Graceland

Elvis hated wearing the jumpsuits, the capes, the scarves, the jewelry, the belt buckles. It was all so weighty, encumbering. He would have rather gone out on stage in jeans and a work shirt. If the people in Vegas didn't like that, that was all right. Elvis didn't need any more money. But as far as Vegas goes, Elvis did need to show that he could outsell anyone there. After his dismal 1956 bombing in Vegas, Elvis needed to know that they had made a mistake. In order to prove that, the Colonel trotted Elvis out in the costumes. Elvis did show all of Las Vegas he could outdraw Sinatra, Dean Martin, Sammy Davis Jr., and anyone else, but the fear of failing never went away. No matter what costume he put on, he was still The Hillbilly Cat underneath.

Of course, the only thing to make it all go away, was for Elvis to change his life so completely that he had to bury the old Elvis, which is what he figuratively did, and is what most people believe he did literally.

So, food and fear were at the center of the whole thing. Elvis used food to feed the old hunger inside, but the food just fed the old fears, namely, that even though Elvis had millions of adoring fans, had every material thing he could want, which he tossed aside or gave away just as soon as he saw something better. All the time Elvis was haunted by the kid growing up in the shotgun house on Old Saltillo Road, on the wrong side of the tracks, illuminated by kerosene lamps, in Tupelo, Mississippi, wondering if his father had gotten fired, would the sheriff come to the door with his deputies to take his father away, would his father make it home with the weekly salary of eighteen dollars he earned at the lumber yard, and would there be enough money for food.

Sometimes there wasn't enough money for food. Sometimes his father didn't make it home. But when Vernon did make it home, when there was enough money, they celebrated like all poor people celebrate making it through another week, they went out and the first thing they bought was food, glorious food. And does Elvis remember shopping for food? Even now, Elvis says that was one of the things he, his mother, and father did together. Saturday late afternoon food shopping. They went to church together, and they went shopping for food together.

Elvis remembers that sometimes, after they got home from shopping, and the bags of groceries were on the kitchen floor and on the table, he would sit down on the floor actually hug the bags of food. Church was church, but for Elvis, the Piggly-Wiggly was a shrine.

Eighteen: Mystery Train

One of the worst ideas Colonel Tom Parker had was to have a train carry a coffin supposedly containing the last mortal remains of Elvis tour the country. Sam Phillips and Elvis nixed the idea right away, but the Colonel fought for his plan right to the bitter end. He could see the financial potential, and anytime the Colonel saw money, he could not let even a bad plan go to waste.

The way he explained it, it would be called the Mystery Train, after Elvis' last record for Sun Records. The Mystery Train would contain the surrogate Elvis body in a state of refrigerated mumificaton pumped full of formaldehyde, his gold records, furniture from Elvis's Jungle Room at Graceland, maybe a few old Caddies and a blue limo. The Mystery Train would start out in Tupelo, make its way to Memphis, then through the Carolinas and eventually to New York where it would remain a week or so. Fans would pay a few dollars to visit what would be an Elvis museum on wheels. There would be a viewing room where people could watch a film on Elvis's life, an insider's look at Graceland, and The Colonel could sell videos of Elvis's various performances. The Colonel would have to talk to Shelby Singleton because Shelby bought Sun Records from Sam Phillips after Sam lost interest in the label and was concentrating on other investments, including being one of the early investors in Holiday Inn back in the '50's. The Colonel said he would talk to Shelby Singleton, and get permission to use the Sun Records label and reissue all the Sun sides because he was certain that Elvis's fans would pay at least $5.00 each per single. The Colonel had been around Graceland often enough to stop in the souvenir shops up and down Elvis Presley Boulevard to know that those early Sun singles were being bootlegged and sold for a handsome profit, and the Colonel didn't want just some of the action. He wanted it all.

Once the crowds slackened in New York, the Colonel would head the Mystery Train to Hollywood. Along the way there would be stops in Philadelphia, Chicago, and, of course, Las Vegas. All of this would take months. Elvis reminded the Colonel that by then any self-respecting corpse would be rotting away. Okay, maybe Elvis had a point, so the Colonel said that everyone should forget about the body, but still keep the idea of having the Mystery Train Travelling Museum.

Of course, with Elvis going into hiding, the Colonel had to think about how he was going to support himself beyond the royalties that RCA would pay, plus his share of money earned by Graceland and Elvis's estate. It took weeks to dissuade the Colonel. After all, his entire life, dating back to his days as a carney, was focused on how to get every suckers' last dime. It caused Col. Tom Parker no amount of anguish to pass up a natural money-making scheme like the Mystery Train.

Finally, Elvis asked The Colonel if he gave him an extra $10,000 a week for the next year, would he drop the plan. After an appropriate amount of wheedling, the Colonel relented, having guaranteed himself an extra half million for the coming year without doing anything for it. This was always the Colonel's favorite kind of money. Money for nothing. However, knowing the Colonel as well as he does, it wouldn't surprise Elvis to learn that the Colonel has rescued a locomotive and passenger cars from a recently defunct rail line and is slowly assembling his dream, The Elvis Presley Mystery Train Travelling Museum Theatre On Wheels, and Elvis Fan Emporium of Rare and Fine Collectibles, coming to a railroad siding near you.

Elvis is surprised that the Colonel hasn't come up with other money-making schemes, like having a 900 number. He can see it now. Dial 1-900-ELVIS4U. All of your questions about Elvis will be answered in the past-tense. Where did he buy his clothes? Was it only Nudie's of Hollywood? What brand of peanut butter did Elvis prefer on his fried banana and peanut butter sandwiches? Everybody knows, if there's a buck to be made, The Colonel will be out there, waving his aluminum cane in the air, walking on arthritic legs in defience of gravity, because even at eighty-three, no one is going to walk away from The Colonel until the master of hoax, homily and hokum has squeezed that sucker dry.

Nineteen: Elvis In Pink & Black or Pop Exam One

1. We know that Elvis's last manager was Col. Tom Parker and that Bob Neal was Elvis's second manager. Who was his first? A rare clue. He was affiliated with Fernwood Records and helped produce Thomas Wayne's million seller, "Tragedy", in 1959.
    Was it:
    1. Jack Clement
    2. Johnny Cash
    3. Scotty Moore
    4. Bill Black
    5. Roy Orbison
    6. Andy Warhol

2. Before the Colonel cut his partner out of handling Elvis, who was going to have a half-share of managing Elvis?
    Was it:
    1. Hank Snow
    2. Eddy Arnold
    3. Minnie Pearl
    4. Ernest Tubb
    5. Joe DiMaggio
    6. Steve Allen

3. Elvis recorded a number of songs since recorded by other artists. Match the original artist with each song.
    1. Money Honey   a. The Ink Spots
    2. I Got A Woman   b. Richard Pennimen
    3. That's When Your Heartaches   c. Hank Snow

Nineteen: Elvis In Pink & Black or Pop Exam One

Begin

4. Blue Moon of Kentucky   d. The Drifters
5. Good Rockin' Tonight   e. Roy Brown
6. Milk Cow Blues   f. Ray Charles
7. Hound Dog   g. Red Foley
8. Tutti Frutti   h. Willie Mae Thornton
9. Old Shep   i. Bill Monroe
10. A Fool Such As I   j. Kokomo Arnold

4. When Elvis arrived for his disastrous performance at the Grand Ole Opry, which country music icon told him he should go back to driving a truck?
   Was it:
   1. Hank Locklin
   2. Hank Thompson
   3. Hank Williams
   4. Hank Snow
   5. Hank Penny

5. Elvis's favorite colors were pink and black. Now they are purple, blue and green. What was the color of the Cadillac Elvis bought for his mother, Gladys?
   1. Black
   2. Mediterranean Blue
   3. White
   4. Pink

5a. Bonus question: Could Gladys Presley drive?
   1. Yes
   2. No

6. Name Elvis's favorite movie star when Elvis was growing up.
   Was it:
   1. Clark Gable
   2. Gene Autry
   3. James Cagney

    4. Jimmy Stewart
    5. Lash LaRue
    6. Cary Grant

7. Name the actor Elvis admires most.
    1. John Wayne
    2. James Dean
    3. Gary Cooper
    4. Marlon Brando
    5. Frankie Avalon

Question One. (3) Scotty Moore, phenom guitarist who knew how to fill in the ends of phrases with sparkling riffs, was Elvis's first manager. He got the bookings for all the early gigs, bought the food for the trips and drove the car. He did it all, which makes it impossible to understand why The Colonel cut Scotty out after a dispute over money. If you answered (6) Andy Warhol, you have a wonderful imagination but if Elvis was even in the same room with Mr. Warhol, Mr. Presley would have decked him and his phoney toupee in a heartbeat.

Question Two. (1) Hank Snow was cut out of the Presley deal. Snow and the Colonel were partners in a management operation that focused on Country & western artists, especially those working on the Louisiana Hayride, where Elvis found his first regular work as a performer. But more about this in Question Four.

Question Three:

(1.) "Money Honey" was first cut by (d) The Drifters

(2.) "I Got A Woman" was written and recorded by (f) by Ray Charles

(3.) "That's When Your Heartaches Begin" was recorded by Billy Bunn, and it's a record that out-Elvis's Elvis. The first recording of "That's When Your Heartaches Begin" was by (a) The Ink Spots.

(4) "Blue Moon of Kentucky" was written and recorded by (i) the father of Bluegrass music, Bill Monroe. Purists still prefer the

September 16, 1946, Monroe recording because of its mournful pace and the exceptional high and lonesome voice of Bill Monroe.

(5) (e) Roy Brown had a number of hits in the '40's and early '50's. "Good Rockin' Tonight" was recorded in the '40's and is transformed into a driving anthem by Wynonie Harris's recording on King Records, in 1948, that turned on the early '50's teenagers, previously known as the Silent Generation, to the evils of Black music and lust, which frightened their parents. Let's face it, what else could Elvis mean when he sang, "Meet me here honey behind the barn, don't cha worry, baby, I won't mean you no harm." After that, it was "Mamas, lock up your daughters." And preachers began to yell from their lofty pulpits about the dangers of this new kind of animalistic Devil's music. And the more they fought it, the hotter it became. Just what would they think when Jerry Lee would say, "You can shake it one time for me,"or "Great Balls of Fire," or "You leave me breathless?" Station managers banned his records from the air and that was even before he married his thirteen year old cousin before divorcing his second, or was that his third wife. They fired his ass the first chance they got.

(6) (j) Kokomo Arnold wrote and sang "Milk Cow Blues" in 1936. "Milk Cow Blues" was also a hit of Bob Wills and His Texas Playboys, in 1946, thinly disguised under the title of "Brain Cloudy Blues". Speaking of Kokomo Arnold, he was a tremendously influencial writer. Some might criticize Elvis for covering Kokomo Arnold, as well as other relatively unknown artists. I suggest that you listen to Kokomo Arnold's "Busy Bootin",

> Busy bootin' and you can't come in,
> Busy bootin' and you can't come in,
> Busy bootin' and you can't come in,
> Come back tomorrow night and try it again.

Then listen to Little Richard's "Keep A Knockin'".

> Keep a knockin' but you can't come in.
> Keep a knockin' but you can't come in.
> Keep a knockin' but you can't come in.
> Come back tomorrow and try it again.

At least Elvis credits Kokomo Arnold with writing the song. Little Richard claims authorship without credit to Arnold. And while I'm at it, when Little Richard cut all those sides down in New Orleans with Dave Bartholomew's Band, on some of the cuts it wasn't even Little Richard on piano, but Huey "Piano" Smith. But, I digress.

(7) (h) "Hound Dog", written by Jerry Leiber and Mike Stoller, was the number one Rhythm & Blues song of the year, in 1953, sung by Willie Mae "Big Mama" Thornton. Hound Dog gave way to Rufus Thomas's answer song "Bear Cat", which was Sun Records first best-seller. Leiber and Stoller went on to write dozens of hits for Elvis, including, "Jailhouse Rock", "Loving You", "Don't", "Treat Me Nice", and "She's Not You", among others.

(8) (b) Elvis covered Richard (Little Richard) Pennimen's "Tutti Frutti".

(9) (g) Red Foley (Pat Boone's father-in-law) had the biggest selling version of "Old Shep" before Elvis cut it. This was an early favorite of Elvis's. He sang it in grade school. Elvis sany "Old Shep" at a county fair singing contest. I often wonder who came in first.

(10) (c) "A Fool Such As I" was a hit for none other than Hank Snow, whose other hits include "I'm Moving On" (recorded by Ray Charles and the Rolling Stones, among others), "Rhumba Boogie", "The Golden Rocket", and "I Don't Hurt Anymore". A lead character in Robert Altman's NASHVILLE was based on Hank. He's the one who talks through his nose and wearing a white toupee that is about two sizes too large., just like the one Hank Snow, The Singing Ranger wore in real life.

That's it for the mix and match section. Now back to our regularly scheduled exam.

Question Four. (4) When Elvis got off stage, it was Hank Snow who told him that he should go back to driving a truck. Of course, Elvis didn't understand the source of the enmity, which was that the Colonel had double-dealed Hank out of his half of Elvis's contract.

Question Five. Elvis bought his mother a pink Caddy, and didn't make no never mind that Gladys couldn't drive. It would sit out in a carport on Audubon Drive. for all the neighbors to see. Does Elvis have a car now? No. Too much paper work. Most states require a photo with each driver's license. Then there is insurance, registration, taxes, and you name it. Elvis havs no licenses, no permanent address, no forms to fill out, and no lines to stand in. He used to think that having more would make him free. Now he knows it's the less you have that makes you free.

Question Six. (5) Without question, Elvis's favorite movie star from his childhood is Lash LaRue, who is still alive. He was even pictured on the back of Johnny Cash's albums before he was canned by Columbia after making money for them for twenty-five years. Lash LaRue, the original man in black, fought crime with a bullwhip. Every cowboy had a sidekick. Lash's was Fuzzy Knight.

Question Seven. (2) Although Elvis admired John Wayne, especially his political views, Elvis thought that James Dean was a most believable actor of his generation, or any generation since. His movies sear with pain, especially "Rebel Without a Cause". Elvis thinks that casting James Dean against Jim Backus as son and father was a mistake. When Dean and Backus have their terrible fight scene, Elvis can't help but remember that Backus was also the voice for Mr. McGoo, the near-sighted bumbling geezer who kept walking into walls and talking to lamps because he thought they were people.

He also likes Gary Cooper movies, especially "High Noon", and "On The Waterfront" with Marlon Brando. As far as Frankie Avalon movies go, Elvis has never seen one, and he hopes that Frankie Avalon has never seen one of his.

That's the end of Pop Exam One. Elvis said I'm squandering my time. He says that if I don't hurry up and end this, he's going to make one of his burnt bacon sandwiches and set off the smoke alarm. Again.

Twenty: Illinois Elvis Sighting

In Springfield, Illinois, the home of Abraham Lincoln, thieves broke into the home of a Muscular Dystrophy poster child. The thieves must have been reading the newspaper and learned that Timothy Larkin and his family were at a dinner honoring Timothy as this year's poster child. When the Larkins returned home, they found that appliances, beds, sports equipment, family photo albums, plumbing, a wood burning stove, "every stitch of clothing we didn't have on our backs," pots and pans, food, one toilet seat, two tvs, lamps, and the thieves also unscrewed light bulbs from ceiling fixtures, everything was gone.

The thieves ransacked Timothy's room. They took his bed, blankets, bureau, his tv, his Nintendo unit and all games. Worst of all, the thieves took the lifesize poster of himself given to him by the Muscular Dystrophy Association.

Mrs. Larkin says that all the things meant something, but that Timothy was really devastated by the loss of the poster. "That really meant a lot to him." The Larkin family had some insurance, but the company said that their policy won't cover the replacement of their losses because the family had limited coverage for personal injury or loss of the house because of fire or other natural causes. The Larkins said that they had minimal insurance on their house and property because of the enormous medical expenses they incur in caring for their son, Timothy. Both Mr. and Mrs. Larkin work two jobs, and work rotating shifts so that one of them is home with Timothy at all times.

Twenty: Illinois Elvis Sighting

The dinner honoring Timothy as the state's poster child was a special event, the first time that the Larkins have been out together in years. There is a five thousand dollar reward established by friends, neighbors, and family of the Larkins for the capture of the thieves. The state Muscular Dystrophy Association has promised the delivery of another poster to Timothy.

After radio, tv, and newspaper reports of the Larkins' situation came to light, area businesses, family friends, church and civic organizations began to replace the furniture and appliances. Donations of food and pledges of money have continued to pour in. Within an hour after the robbery had been reported on the 10:00 evening news, people arrived at the Larkins' home carrying furniture, bedclothes, cooking utensils, and money. "It was a real community outpouring," said Lt. John Monahan, who was still at the scene near midnight when the donations started to arrive. By two a.m., beds had arrived and had been set up so that the Larkins could get some sleep. But people kept coming to their home with canned goods, fresh fruit and vegetables, donuts, boxes of toys and appliances.

It was around two a.m. that a long, blue limousine with tinted glass and Tennessee license plates rolled up in front of the Larkins' home. The driver got out and opened the right rear door. There were two people inside. "We could make out their shadows," Mrs. Larkin said. One of the men handed the driver several boxes. The driver carried the boxes to the Larkins' front door. He asked if anyone was a member of the Larkin family, since there were about a dozen people at the front of the house. Mrs. Larkin identified herself, and the driver handed a box labeled Super Nintendo to her. He placed the other boxes on the cement porch and returned to the car. More boxes were passed to the driver, who returned to the Larkins' porch and placed the boxes down. "For Timothy," he said.

The driver returned to the car, opened the trunk and removed a large box containing a television. He struggled back to the

Larkins' porch. "For Timothy," he said, "with our best wishes." The driver returned to the car. A man in the back of the limousine leaned forward and waved. Then the driver closed the right rear door, walked behind the limo, got in the driver's seat and drove off.

Mr. Larkin, who had been summoned from inside the house, got a glimpse of the man. Mrs. Larkin was unable to speak. A neighbor was able to jot down a portion of the license plate as the limousine drove slowly into the chilly January night. The numbers were __-30726. A computer check with the Tennessee State Police listed no motor vehicle with that license plate. A few days later, a diehard Elvis fan happened to be rereading a book called ELVIS WORLD by Jane and Michael Stern. On page 36 there is a picture of Vernon and Gladys Presley standing in their driveway between two Cadillacs. The one on the left has the license number 2D-30726. The fan, who wishes to remain anonymous, gave the information to the police, then to the news media. The editor at the city desk at the Springfield *Times* told her that the similarity in the number sequence of the two license plates was only a coincidence. The woman who discovered the coincidence decided not to pursue the matter further. She is a grammar school teacher in Springfield and didn't want to be labeled as a kook, one of those loonies you read about in the super market check-out line tabloids who claim to have seen Elvis.

I checked with Elvis. He said as far as he knew the license plate was on another car, at Graceland, but you know how fans are, everything gets stolen.

And where was Elvis when this incident occurred? In a hunting lodge north of Weir, Maine. We were together the entire time. Honest.

By way of an addendum to the previous chapter. After showing the Pop Exam to Elvis, he said he had never heard Roy Brown's version of "Good Rockin' Tonight". The one he heard was by

Twenty: Illinois Elvis Sighting

Wynonie Harris, which came out the same year as Roy Brown's original, but sold more copies.

Elvis wants to know what an addendum is. I tell him it's an addition to something previously said. "Oh," he says, "probably what you need there instead is an erratum." I immediately know I'm wrong, but I don't say anything. He's hard enough to live with when I'm right.

Twenty-One: Pricilla & Elvis

Elvis and I are heading for the Brunch Bar, a place we like, in Windsor, Vermont. I'm driving because I'm certain that the way Elvis drives we'll get pulled over, and Elvis has no license. Let me tell you how he drives. Sometimes he drives ten miles an hour in a thirty-five mile zone. He can't concentrate. If he's talking to someone, he has to face them, whether they're sitting next to him or sitting in the back seat. I've seen him take his eyes off the road for what seemed like minutes at a time, trying to make a point about something. He thinks he's protected by some higher authority. That's why I do the driving.

We got Reba McEntire playing on the tape deck, "He Broke Your Memory Tonight", co-written by Dicky Lee, another Sun Records alumnus, who wrote "She Thinks I Still Care" for George Jones. Elvis turns the volume down and says, "Bob Lamb." I ask him, "What?" Elvis says Bob Lamb was the guy who recorded "That's When Your Heartaches Begin". At least he thinks that's his name.

"When I saw Billy Bunn on your list last night, I couldn't place the name. Are you sure he recorded "That's When Your Heartaches Begin" ? Elvis asks.

I tell him I'm sure, he recorded for Victor. Elvis says he doesn't remember the name. Then he says, "I wonder how many other things you screwed up on your quizzes." I tell him that it doesn't matter because no one is going to believe that you're still alive, so what does a few slightly off answers on a quiz matter. "Plenty," he says, "you got to get it right, especially those musicians. Give credit where credit is due. Guys like Bob Lamb and Roy Brown never got a break. Back in the Sixties I ran into Roy Brown. I don't know exactly where. I think it was in Little Rock. They were having an Elvis Presley Day, or something. Roy Brown wanted to see me but they wouldn't let him in. They didn't know who he was; you know, just another Black guy. So he wrote me a note, said that he was my yardman and wanted to know what work I wanted him to do.

"I got the note and went out to see him. He was broke and in trouble with the I.R.S. I can see Willie Nelson and Jerry Lee in trouble with them, but Roy Brown never made it. He said he didn't have anything the IRS could take. And you know how those publishing companies can screw you. I wrote him a check for everything he needed and then some. Hell, he's the guy who wrote 'Good Rockin' Tonight'. You can't put a number on how much I owe him. So, it's those forgotten guys, the guys like Smiley Lewis, Arthur Crudup, Amos Milburn, Faye Adams, Doug Poindexter, and Hardrock Gunter who work in the shadows, and who should have made it. You got to get it right, so they don't get forgotten."

We park near the Windsor Post Office and walk a block to the Brunch Bar. Along the way we see J.D. Salinger. He lives across the river, in Cornish. Like Elvis, he's another recluse from the 1950's. Thin and gray, wearing glasses, he's on his way to the Post Office. I wonder if he's going to buy some Elvis stamps. We nod hello as we pass each other. No sense trying to ask if he's writing anything. J.D. is stone deaf and wouldn't hear us.

Once inside the Brunch Bar, Elvis and I order scrambled eggs and ham with a side of home fries. The waitress brings us our coffee. Suddenly, I know we're in trouble. She gives one of those "I know who you are" looks, then gives "but I won't say anything" smiles. I watch her as she goes back behind the counter. She writes something down in her order book, but she doesn't say anything to the rest of the help. So we're safe for a few minutes.

"What is this thing with waitresses?" I ask Elvis.

"I don't know, man. Let's talk about something else."

Elvis has been reading ELVIS AND ME, a book written by Pricilla Beaulieu Presley, with Sandra Harmon. I ask Elvis what he thinks about the book. That "with Sandra Harmon" is a mighty big "with"', Elvis says. I don't ever remember kissing Pricilla's "carefully parted lips." I ask him what he's talking about. He says there's a line in the book where he kisses Pricilla's "carefully-parted lips." It's a direct quote from the book. Elvis is not outraged but finds the book funny. Yes, he says, a lot of the things in the book are true, including Pricilla's weird hair-do, dyeing it black, smoking dope and stuff, "but I wasn't into anything weird, like tying her up." The book has some truth, but you can take an event and color it anyway you want. Elvis says, "I think this book is more Sandra Harmon than Pricilla. My guess is that Pricilla talked into a tape recorder about our life together and her ghost writer filled in the colors. You know," Elvis says smiling, "I could write a book about it and it would come out differently. I'd come out sweet, and I could say some damaging things, but what would be the point? It's my life and it's nobody's business what went on. Besides I'm not running for president. They guy we got in there now never dodged the draft, never inhaled, and never made the double-backed beast with Jennifer Flowers. I've got no time for the past."

"Making the double-backed beast?" I ask. "What's that about?"

"That's Shakespeare, my man," Elvis says. "You see, I'm just not the same man I was, and I was hardly the man Pricilla writes about in her book."

We eat our breakfast. It's great. Elvis has only one complaint. They use oleo on the toast rather than butter.

"You know," Elvis says, "Fate is a strange thing. You can work hard, have a ton of talent, and still fate decides everything. Take Carl Perkins. I couldn't write songs, but Carl could and still does. He could play guitar better than just about anyone. But my version of "Blue Suede Shoes probably gets played more than his. It's all fate. Take Pricilla and me. We lived together and she was underage, fifteen, going to high school. We kept it quiet, even

Twenty-One: Pricilla & Elvis

though I was surrounded by reporters. Jerry Lee Lewis marries a young girl and they crucified him. Of course, his problem was he didn't have the organization in front of him, and he's not the smartest person in the world. I don't think he has an ounce of guile in him. When it came time to talk to the press, he and his wife were out there all alone, cornered. And Jerry Lee compounded the problem by telling those reporters the truth, that his wife is his cousin, that he had been married three or four times before, that one was a shotgun wedding, and at one time he had been married to two women at the same time.

"Can you imagine that? That was the end of him. Dick Clark dropped him like a hot penny. It's easy to see why Jerry Lee Lewis turned mean. If he couldn't trust those close to him, he pushed them away. And why did it happen to him instead of me? Fate. That's all it was."

"But you've got to admit, he didn't help himself."

"His first mistake was being honest. Bill Clinton wouldn't be president if he were honest. Didn't inhale. I don't know about you, but I don't trust anyone who doesn't inhale," Elvis says, smiling.

"And Pricilla's book?" I ask. "Truth or fiction?"

"There is an element of truth. It's all perception, then filled in by the ghost writer. But there's one thing I hope nobody else catches."

"What's that?"

"The Books. Pricilla notices that all my books are gone when she goes back to Graceland. I should have left the books on the shelf, but I took things in a hurry, things that meant a lot to me. I should have left everything just as it was. I didn't think that Pricilla would come back to Graceland and go upstairs to my rooms. We had cleaned them up before the mock funeral. I don't know why. We should have left them the way they were. I just hope nobody else catches that."

We finish breakfast and head back to the car. It's nearly noon, cold, but the sun is bright. We're going over to Woodstock, a winding forty-five minute drive from here. They're having an antique car exposition at the Woodstock Inn and on the Town Green. Elvis just has to go. What's strange is that the Cadillacs that he bought new in 1956 and 1957 are now considered antiques. Elvis goes to car meets a lot. There is something about the old cars, heavier and longer than some whales, that intrigues Elvis. When he was growing up, that was success. You get yourself a Cadillac and float down the street, you and everybody you know just knows you have made it. Try that with a Toyota! No contest. In those distant, halcyon days, success was measured by how much you could consume, and those Caddies, how they could consume.

Back at the lodge, Elvis reads what I've written and asks what "halcyon" means. I tell him, "peaceful, free of care." "Sorry," he says, "you've got the wrong word, man. I haven't had a halcyon day since 1953 or 54." The he suggests that I get Sandra Harmon to write this for me, which, in the Elvis scale of things, is like saying Robert Goulet is one of your favorite singers, a performer whose smarmy style caused Elvis to shoot out televisions in at least three states.

Twenty-Two: Wish I Was In Heaven Sitting Down

The important news today is that Bill Clinton is going to end the ban against gays in the military, is going to end cost of living increases for people on social security, will have to put off his middle class tax break, and will start looking for a new candidate for Attorney General. Andre the Giant died in Paris. He was in France to attend his father's funeral when he suffered a heart attack.

Elvis likes wrestling. Sure, he knows it's phony, but what isn't? His favorite wrestler is The Undertaker, a four hundred pound grim reaper whose favorite move is the Tombstone, where he crashes his victim head first into the mat, rendering him totally unconscious. It's at this point that The Undertaker's manager, Paul Bearer, carries an urn and a body bag into the ring. The unconscious wrestler is slipped into the body bag and then the bag is zipped, much to the horror or delight of the attending wrestling fans.

Elvis says wrestling is like opera; dramatic, but the wrestlers are so acrobatic. Their timing is impeccable. Sure, everyone knows who's going to win, but everyone knows who's going to die in Shakespeare and triumph in opera. Knowing how a thing is going to turn out doesn't necessarily diminish the pleasure of the event.

Professional wrestling is the new moral drama, good versus evil, just like the old westerns of Elvis's childhood. White hat versus black hat, except when it came to Lash LaRue, the good man wearing black everything. When Hulk Hogan wrestled Colonel Mustafa, an Iranian waving his country's flag around the ring while Americans were being held hostage, is a perfect example.

Elvis prefers watching matches promoted by the World Wresting Federation instead of Ted Turner's group made up of wrestlers who aren't good enough to make it in the WWF, or had-beens who used to belong to the WWF. But now that The Hulkster has gone into retirement, the WWF has been hard-pressed to find a champion to replace him as a money maker. The Ultimate Warrior was a contender, but he didn't have it.

Elvis says that the wrestling has gotten so dull that he sometimes watches Larry King. More good versus evil. Same with Oprah and Jerry Springer. Even more good versus evil. Elvis says that compared to Larry, Oprah, and Jerry Springer, WWF wrestling is real. Elvis doesn't watch that much tv. Maybe an hour after a late supper. He's usually in bed by eleven. He has finished Lao Tzu and has begun THE CLOUD OF UNKNOWING.

Fortunately, Elvis never discusses his religious views with me. He feels that if he studies long enough, he'll understand why we're all here. I put on my headphones, listen to Dr. Ross, and read Peter Guralnick's FEEL LIKE GOING HOME. Is there a better writer about music? Nick Tosches is out there. How about William Ferris? Or Robert Palmer? And I never can get enough of Stanley Booth.

You might think it strange, but Elvis will not read anything about music, and certainly not anything about himself. It only makes him angry. So many writers who didn't know him with their assumptions. Even Pricilla's book, which he merely scanned, he says was wrong-minded because Pricilla let the ghost-writer make all the conclusions. Jerry Hopkins, on the other hand, probably came closest to the truth without knowing it. Elvis says that those writers should go to Chicago or Mississippi and write about the old blues guys who still use a bottleneck when they play guitar. That's where the real music history is. How about writing about Rev. Robert Wilkins. That guy's been singing for fifty years, playing an old beat up guitar with a pen-knife, singing "I Wish I Was In Heaven Sitting Down", or "Lord, I Want You To Help Me." Nobody writes about him. Rev. Robert Wilkins might

Twenty-Two: Wish I Was In Heaven Sitting Down

be dead for all we know. Just more music history lost that no one will know. What a waste.

Elvis says that when he's about seventy, he's going to record an album of spirituals, just him on guitar and piano. Of course, he'll use another name. Maybe something like Blind Mississippi Lonesome Sundown or maybe the Reverend Big Daddy Sweetwater. Would Elvis sing, "I Wish I Was In Heaven Sitting Down?" "Hell, no," he says. "When I get to Heaven, I'm going to jump around. Man, in that sweet by and by." And Elvis starts humming at first, then quietly sings the words, so no one outside this room will hear him. "When that final trumpet sounds, I'll be getting up and walking round. Ain't no grave can hold my body down."

When he finishes singing low, I ask him where he heard that song. "It's old," he said. "I don't know where it came from. It's one of those songs you hear all your life. Probably goes back before time. Maybe an old slave song, because you know that good church-going white people wouldn't be getting up and walking round. They figure they'll be in Heaven before anyone, sitting quietly, waiting for their wings. Brother, do they have a surprise coming."

We look at each other and laugh at the irony. Like either of us has a chance to get to Heaven. As Mark Twain said, "Heaven for propriety, the other place for society."

Twenty-Three: Code Seven Red Alert-Interdiction Hell Fire-The Plan To Kill Elvis

When something bad happens, it happens in a hurry. The crash. Something against the door before it's splintered. Police in riot gear are all over the apartment, pushing me down and out of the way. They check with each other about who I am and how much I know. And it's clear, especially to me, that I'm in deeper than I know about what's going on.

There is one man, plain clothes, talking in code about jurisdiction. Four men come into the room. I recognize two of them. People I've talked to in the past few months about Memphis and music in general, and Elvis specifically. People I wouldn't have guessed are connected with some branch of security or the government.

Everything has gone crazy. I'm hauled in front of a man I talked with two years ago who passed himself off as an insurance agent who collected baseball cards. He tells his people that I'm okay, and they literally throw me through a wall that is actually a panel that leads to red carpeted stairs. It's here I realize that the apartment is no ordinary place randomly picked by Elvis as a place to hide out, but has been "prepared" in case of a hit.

And where is Elvis through all this? I have no idea. When the shooting starts, it's softer, quieter than I expect. Little popping sounds. Apparently two factions are fighting. One to protect and the other to take over. I'm huddled down behind the fake wall,

Twenty-Three: Code Seven

scared, like this could be it. I'm clearly into something more involved and dangerous than I could have imagined.

All this time I thought everything was cool. Just Elvis and me cruising in New England. Of course, all the time he's worried about being recognized, and I think it's because of his fans, but it's so much more than that. It's clear at that moment that there have been people watching us, one group to protect and the other to attack.

And suddenly someone is coming down the stairs. My heart is pounding in my ears. A cannister is fired. Gray smoke. And I'm out in a second. My first whiff of something called Robot-Boss gas, something developed for civilian use by the FBI in a plant in Maryland. It's called Robot-Boss gas because it's so insidious that not only will it paralyze the nervous system of humans and animals, it will also "freeze" the circuits of a computer.

I learn later that Robot-Boss gas was designed to paralyze a human temporarily while he or she remained conscious. Sort of like a strong stun gun. But more research is definitely needed because the stuff knocks you out so fast, you're out of it before you hit the floor.

The next morning I come to. I hear different voices, maybe four, standing over me. I'm sitting on the floor. There's something dry in my mouth, like maybe a handkerchief. I hoping a clean handkerchief. My eyes are covered by something soft, like fur, so I can't see or speak. My hands and legs are not tied. They don't have to be. If I decide to run, where would I go? Into which wall?

"You, you awake?" some guy grouses, like he's hoping I'm still out, or worse. "You, we're getting you otta here. No trouble, understand? You're gonna be all right just as long as you listen and don't screw around because me and Mack here are very impatient with people who don't listen. Next time you come to, you're going to be very far from here. I ain't telling how or where, but you'll know when you get there. Understand? You're going to wake up in a safe house. You're job is to shut up about

Elvis. Understand? You saw nothing you know nothing and you say nothing.

I think they expect an answer, so I nod. I don't know who these people are. Friend or enemy? But since I'm still alive, I'll guess the former.

"We're taking you outta here. You understand? One wrong move and it's over, understand? I nod, yes. "You gotta forget everything, and you gotta keep your mouth shut. We work for Elvis. He's gone. He's left the building, you got it. Some problems came up and you're one of the problems, and none of this is any of your business, *Capishe*? Just do what I say."

I don't ask anything, like, "who are you, what happened, or where's Elvis?" I am in total, complete, irretrievable fear for my life. What I'm up against here?

"Okay, we're leaving soon. Mack packed some of your stuff. If you're wondering if you'll see Elvis again, I doubt it. Nothing to be gained. He's got to be real careful now. You were a good decoy, but you're not useful anymore. We could get rid of you, but Elvis said, no, so you gotta thank him. I mean, pal, if I had my way, and he makes a sound of something getting his throat cut.

I listen to them carefully as I feel someone leaning over me, breathing on me. They say nothing. I wonder what's nest, then I feel a needle going into my left arm.

I'm given another dose of Robot-Boss gas and I'm gone, dreaming nitrous oxide dentist dreams, sodium pentathol dreams, dreams of wars and famines in Croatia and Somalia, sepia visions of blown-up cities and starving faces, the problem so huge it defies comprehension. Four hundred Palestinian detainees kicked out of Palestine twice, while the voices of Larry King and Senator Lautenberg of New Jersey say it's all right because the detainees could go back to Israel and ask for a fair trial. A jury is being selected in the second Rodney King trial. Someone is investigating poisoned chickens in the Pacific Northwest. Marge Schott is suspended for a year and fined $25,000 for making racist and anti-semetic remarks, a decision spear-headed by the Reverend

Twenty-Three: Code Seven

Jesse Jackson, who, by his own admission, used to spit in white people's food when he worked at a restaurant, and while he was running for president of the United States called New York "Hymietown." Then there's an ad for a natural laxative. When I open my eyes, I'm exactly where I don't want to be. I'm in a strange house or apartment. The tv's tuned to CNN. All I can think of is that Gil Scott-Heron said that the revolution will not be televised, but it already is. And my head hurts like it's been cleaved by Jeffrey Dahmer and put back together with crazy glue.

Twenty-Four: Two Trains Running

In Joseph Campbell's HERO WITH A THOUSAND FACES, he writes that Orpheus, or any of the Gods, may be walking down 42nd Street, standing in a doorway panhandling, or voluntarily washing your windshield with a crumpled newspaper while you're stuck in traffic. We never know where or when we'll encounter the Gods next or what form they will take. I am in New Orleans in the apartment that belonged to Roy Byrd, as least that is what I'm told. Roy Byrd used to be known as Professor Longhair, and he was legendary in this city of musical legends.

I got down here by a modern version of the underground railway run by what I'll call the blues Musicians Benevolent Association, or Shim Sham Shimmy. When I woke up, I was here. Two musicians from Fats Domino's band live in the Professor's old place. They say, "No names, please."

The apartment has a living room filled with musical instruments: a baby grand piano, a set of drums, and two saxes resting on top of the piano, one alto and one tenor. Whenever I ask how I got here, the subject gets changed. They all talk quietly. A recording of Billy "The Kid" Emerson is playing, "When It Rains, It Really Pours". One of the musicians says that they're just holding me until they get the word that's all right for me to go. Again, I don't ask about Elvis. He doesn't exist. This is an edgy situation. I can tell that the two men are uncomfortable about having me here. They give me a plate of blackened catfish and a can of Diet Pepsi, then they wander off into the a corner of the room and talk quietly.

Twenty-Four: Two Trains Running

While I'm eating the blackened catfish, a large man, about 300 hundred pounds of mountainous blubber, comes into the apartment. The three men talk and motion toward me. The large man comes over and introduces himself as Big Chief Jolly, but it's assumed that that's not his real name.

"You got to come with me," he says. I get up, place my plate on a table, and we go out into the night. A car is waiting for us. Maybe a '68 Pontiac. We drive around without talking. Then Big Chief says, "We got all your stuff. Someone dropped the tape recorder, but all your notes and equipment are in the trunk. Nobody brought your clothes or personal stuff. We brought what we thought was important."

"Thanks."

Big Chief says, "I suppose you want to know what happened two days ago. Well, I don't know anything. I'm just a stop along the way. I'm not sure you were worth saving, but you were there. Either they get you or we get you."

"Who are they?" I ask.

"Forget it, Cracker. Nobody's going to say nothing. That's the only way to survive. Just enjoy the ride. I'm putting you on a train to Memphis. After that, I don't care what happens to you."

"But I don't have any money."

The chief gives me a long look from up high. "Man, you got a mother, a friend somewhere? Have them wire you some money. Do I look like the Salvation Army?"

"No, but..."

"But, nothin'. Look, you don't know how lucky you are. I'm just supposed to drop you off, and I'm taking a chance. It's not something I wanna do, you know what I mean? Someone along the line thinks you're okay, so I'm doing my part, so why don't you use your head, you know? I mean, I've got things I'd rather do. If it was up to me I would have dumped you down at the docks yesterday. So just chill."

I don't say anything for the rest of the ride. The car stops off at the train station. We get out. Everything is in one blue Nike duffle bag. I head into the station and I don't look back. I check out the train schedule heading north. I go over to the news stand and buy a copy of the *Times-Picayune.* A bus has crashed into a mountain in Mexico, oil spill off the coast of Louisiana, a barge is stuck in ice on the Mississippi, ethnic cleansing continues in eastern Europe, the Dow-Jones is up 33.40, in heavy trading, Dear Abby warns us to have safe sex, and two people die from eating hamburgers at Jack In The Box. What a comfort it is to get word that the world is still normal. I sit down on a bench, read the paper, occasionally glance up at the large clock, doing one of my favorite things: waiting for a train.

Twenty-Five: Extra-Terrestrial Elvis Sighting

I'm back in Memphis drinking with a bunch of musicians whose names you'd recognize, but......

More news about Zoe Baird, the Aetna attorney who makes more than a half a million dollars a year, finally paid her overdue fish bill of $42.11 owed from last year. The check was dated December 10, and the envelope was postmarked February 1. 1993. There is a different set of laws for the rich. We hope this is the last we hear of Clinton's former appointee for Attorney General.

The most recent Elvis sighting was by a woman who was abducted by an alien ship she claims was piloted by Elvis. The woman has since given birth to twins who look like the Everly Brothers.

I have been trying to understand the events from last week. That was a strange break from a relatively quiet life. I don't know why I was kidnapped and shipped down to New Orleans. I haven't mentioned a thing to anyone in town, although Memphis is the natural place you'd find yourself talking about Elvis. I've been putting my notes together. As you might have guessed, a lot of the material is missing. The tape recorder is intact, but the tapes with Elvis talking about his favorite movies, tv shows, and musicians are gone. Just for the record, Elvis loves to watch Christmas movies, especially "It's A Wonderful Life," "Miracle On 34th Street", Jean Shepherd's "A Christmas Story," and "The Bishop's Wife." He owned studio copies of those movies and liked to watch them throughout the year. He thought "Citizen Kane" was a terrific movie, but couldn't watch it more than once a year. He loves "Fried Green Tomatoes" and "A River Runs Through It." There was a little movie house in White River Juction that was showing it, and Elvis went to see it four days in a row.

Elvis's favorite tv show is the "Andy Griffith Show." He said he wished he could find a town like Mayberry and an aunt like Aunt Bea. Elvis likes mysteries, especially Rumpole on PBS and Sherlock Holmes starring Jeremy Brett on A & E. Other than that, Elvis doesn't have patience for tv. He might watch CNN just to catch up on the news, but he seldom watches tv for more than an hour at a time.

The musicians he still listens to include Jerry Reed, Johnny Bond, Johnnie Lee Wills, Bob Wills, Nat King Cole Trio, early Ray Charles, Lil Hardin Armstrong, and Django Reinhardt. Elvis can't figure out how Reinhardt could play those great runs with all five fingers, much less with three fingers that were fused together when he was severely burned in a fire. Elvis plays Miles Davis's "Kind Of Blue" over and over. And as difficult as it might be to imagine, Elvis's late night music often is Jean Pierre Rampal's "Japanese Melodies for Flute and Harp".

When we drove around, he liked to listen to Johnny Cash, Muddy Waters, Beausoleil, or Western Swing. He loves the fiddle work of Johnny Gimble on the Tiffany Transcriptions of Bob Wills and The Texas Playboys. He said it was all good travelling music. And I miss that.

I figure I was given a ticket to Memphis for a reason, so I plan to stick around Memphis for awhile and look up some old friends, like Sam Phillips, Rufus Thomas and Furry Lewis. I can finish a piece on the history of Beale Street Between The Wars I've been working on for six years. just to keep my mind busy. Write about Arthur "Big Boy" Crudup; Sam Chatman, the last of The Mississippi Shieks; Roosevelt Sykes; Sunnyland Slim; Big Joe Williams; or Little Brother Montgomery. All these people gone before I got here, but Beale Street is rich in history. All you have to do is become a music archeologist, set down in one place, don't worry about tomorrow, and just let people on Hernando and Beale streets talk. You could write a history no one's every heard in thirty days. Baldwin wrote IF BEALE STREET COULD TALK. Beale Street has been talking a long time, just now a few people are starting to listen. And I'll stick around. It's cold up north right now. Come to think of it, it's cold up north any time you go there.

Twenty-Six: Ex-Playboy Bunny Recruit Rejects Attorney General Post

Now that the Beverly Hillbillies have moved to Washington and changed their names to Clinton, it is impossible to live in America and not be supplied with daily laughs. This morning's Memphis *Press-Scimitar* reports that Federal Judge Kimba Wood, President Clinton's latest nominee for Attorney General, withdrew her name because she, too, had hired illegal aliens. Jesus, how many illegal aliens are there? It was also revealed that Ms. Wood "trained" as a Playboy Bunny when whe was a student in London in the 1960's. Hey, wait a minute. Wasn't it in London in the late 1960's that Bill Clinton "experimented" with marijuana" I wonder if Kimba Wood and Bill knew each other then.

Another question I have is: just exactly how do you "train" to become a Playboy Bunny? Do they teach you to sit a certain way so you don't squash your cotton-tail? And just how do you stuff your big, old curvy self in that tiny satin, high hip-riding cocktail uniform? I wonder if Kimba listed her Playboy training on her resume. I mean, that little extra experience could give her the edge over other judges who Clinton could have selected for Attorney General One man's meat.

Bill Clinton asked Kimba Wood if she had "the Zoe Baird problem (soon to be written up in the New England Journal of

Medicine)," and it was reported that Kimba denied him three times. Not only is Kimba Wood willing to violate the law, but is equally willing to lie face to face to the president, the qualitites we have come to expect

from Attorney Generals specifically, and politicians in general.

Anyway, it's a warm, sunny winter morning in Memphis. I spent the night with some musician friends I've known from the last days of Sun Records, in the late '60's, just catching up on each other: who's still in music, who's gone back home to Arkansas painting houses, and, of course, who has died. That list gets longer with accelerated speed. Orbison's gone. Hard to believe. That life of tragedy. He wrote "Claudette" for the Everly Brothers about his wife, Claudette, who soon after died in a motorcycle accident. He lost two sons, someone says, in a fire. Roy had remarried and his records were selling again, formed a group with Bob Dylan and George Harrison called the Travelling Wilburys; cut a great video with James Burton. Everything finally going right. Then he's gone. All taken away so suddenly. God is like that.

I think of the few years Roy Orbison cut records for Sun Records. "Except for his recording of "Ooby Dooby" Roywas one musician Sam couldn't get. He tried to be a rocker in the southwest, Buddy Holly mold, but it wasn't working. Johnny Cash, of the coal chute gravelly voice, told Roy that he should try to sing lower. In a few years after leaving Sun, Roy had hit after hit singing higher than ever.

Ray Smith, Earl Peterson, and Bill Black are long gone. Sonny Burgess is selling shoes in Arkansas. At least, that is the most recent news. Scotty Moore has a recording studio in Nashville and still has not forgiven Elvis for dumping him. Sleepy LaBeef, Charlie Feathers, and Carl Perkins are still on the road, spreading the gospel of Sun Records. And the rest of us, those young punks who arrived in Memphis, hypnotized by the spinning 45 rpm logo on Sun Records, what can we say for ourselves? We could have been contenders, but for the gods who smile down on only a few. So, we look at ourselves, tell old stories that have gotten larger and funnier over the years. How could we have taken those giant leaps back then? Quit our jobs, hit the road, believe that we could write music and sing well enough to make a living and even to make a fortune.

Well, that was the dream of our generation. And Memphis was its Mecca. Now we gather and enjoy each other and we celebrate our survival, because, looking back, that, too, was a longshot, as we sit around Alfred's Restaurant on Beale Street in the land of plenty: plenty of poverty, plenty of illegal aliens, plenty of Ted Kennedy wannabes, plenty of jobs leaving the country, in a time of bad air and bad music, but as always; at least we are still free.

Twenty-Seven: Brain Cloudy Day

Pop Quiz Number Five
   Who was the first person to record Elvis?
   Was it:
      1. Jack Clement
      2. Marion Keisker
      3. Sam Phillips
      4. Dewey Phillips
      5. Jud Phillips
      6. Phil Spector

As a result of the recent events, I've had to rethink the reasons for Elvis to go into hiding in the summer of 1977. Obviously, some of the rumors about mob elements, the Federal Witness Protection Program, and Elvis's commitment to Colonel Tom Parker, who has been running up a tab in Vegas for years, come to mind. And, of course, there could be other factors that no one on the outside is aware of. My concern is whether Elvis made it out of the raid all right. There are two people I can contact to learn if he is okay, but they might not be aware of the raid on the apartment. So, it's mostly wait and see.

I've been spending much of my time in Memphis at the places Elvis knows about, with some of his pre-RCA friends. I've been careful not to bring up Elvis in any conversation, and have merely listened when he is mentioned.

Pop Quiz Number Six

Everyone knows that Elvis liked to go to a funeral home at night to look at corpses. Question is, which of the following started a music career by working in a funeral parlor. Was it:

1. Sam Phillips
2. Elton John
3. Madonna
4. Joni Mitchell
5. Ross Perot

Aside from spending time at Alfred's, I've been catching up on Memphis politics at Biggun's Sports Grill. It seems that if you have political clout or a connection to the mob, you never have to worry about being kept in jail or being found guilty in Memphis. For example, I'm told that there are more than three dozen incidents and related charges against Jerry Lee Lewis, in Memphis. The chances that Jerry Lee will ever have to spend time in jail are less than zero. Even when he was arrested for waving a gun at the gates of Graceland, the judge threw the case out.

I find that people here have a lot of affection for Jerry Lee Lewis. They can understand him. He is essentially a working stiff who is too direct, too honest, and that's what they say gets him in trouble. Having been in the same room with Jerry Lee and warching him suddenly punch somebody or break a bottle and threaten to cut up people who stop by to say how great he is, I would have to say that it's more than just being honest that gets him into trouble. But all that doesn't matter. Jerry Lee belongs to Memphis. He has been connected with Memphis for nearly thirty years. He's been here since Eisehower. He is not remote. When his sons, Steve Allen Lewis, and Jerry Lee, Jr. died, everyone knew about it. When his wife ran off with the "dago" detective Jerry Lee hired to follow her, everyone knew about that, too. So, right here, in the Home of the Blues, Elvis might be the Idol, but Jerry Lee Lewis is Everyman.

Twenty-Seven: Brain Cloudy Day

Now for the answers to Pop Quizzes Number Five and Six. Although Cowboy Jack Clement was the engineer at Sun for years, and Sam Phillips did most of the early recording himself, Dewey Phillips, no relation to Sam, is the man who first played Elvis on his radio show, "Red, Hot & Blue," and Jud Phillips, Sam's brother, who went on to manage Jerry Lee Lewis's career, and Phil Spector who extended Sun Records slapback echo into his Wall of Sound, it was Marion Keisker, all-around Sun book keeper, scheduler, comptroller who decided to record Elvis so Sam could hear him while Elvis was cutting his $4.00 disc of "My Happiness" for his mother Gladys.

I'm told that Sam Phillips takes exception to this version, but it is clear that Sam was away. Someone had to record Elvis so he could hear it. Does it matter? Sam's in the Rock and Roll Hall of Fame. Marion kept Sun Records going. She was there when Elvis walked in. The edge goes to Marion.

Question Six. Although Ross Perot looks like an undertaker, and Elton John looks like he's going to visit one soon, and Joni Mitchell writes like one, and Madonna sings like one, it is Sam C. Phillips who early on worked in a funeral parlor. I found this little tidbit in a book I bought today called GOOD ROCKIN' TONIGHT, by Colin Escott with Martin Hawkins. The book has the Sun Record logo on the cover and has a forward by Peter Gurlanick Chapter One is about Sam Phillips. Memphis, and Beale Street, with great photos. It's one of those books that you read and say to yourself, like I'm saying to myself, "Why didn't you write about this? You know all the music and most of the people. Another great idea not acted on." But at least the book exists.

Twenty-Eight: Another Elvis

I'm having a late breakfast at Biggun's. I finished reading GOOD ROCKIN' TONIGHT, but some of Sun's more intriguing musicians have been omitted. Memory is not a durable thing. It has an elasticity that stretches like a fine membrane over our lives. The more it stretches, the more it distorts, and fewer and fewer details are remembered in the same light and context in which they occurred. Eventually, everything will be forgotten and we will have no choice but to invent what never occurred. Most of the material in GOOD ROCKIN' TONIGHT is dead solid, but at this stage most of us old guys can't remember anything right. We start remembering the way we think it should have been rather the the way it happened. The book doesn't even mention Hunki Dori, the Four Dukes, the Five Tinos, Handy Jackson, Eddie Snow, Hot Shot Love or Tracy Pendarvis and The Swampers.

I'm poking around with my scrambled eggs and sausage, reading the *Press-Scimitar* when a young kid with a guitar, sideburns, and a swagger appears out of no where. He is the spitting image of a young Elvis, right on down to his D.A. There is no place for him to sit down, so I signal him to come over and join me. He is youthfully grateful. It turns out that he is one of the United States Postal Service's Elvises that they've hired for a month to sing Elvis songs in Knoxville, Nashville, Chattanooga, Memphis, and other towns throughout Tennessee. Tomorrow his month is up, but he has no intention of going home, which is Tulsa. He's going to stay around and try to land a contract.

Twenty-Eight: Another Elvis

His real name is Louis Krantz but he has changed it as he says, "for perfessional reasons." He has sent demos and left messages at a number of recording studios. He has tried to call Sam Phillips to audition for him, maybe even produce him. Louis Krantz is about thirty years too late. Sam did produce Ricky Nelson's last session before he died, and possibly produced Class of '55, with Carl Perkins, Roy Orbison, and Jerry Lee Lewis. But people forget that Sam is in his seventies, although he doesn't look or act it. I suspect Sam has made a pact with the devil and has a decaying portrait of himself among the rows of boots in one of his closets.

I ask the Louis Krantz what he's changed his name to. He says it's Elvis. He had it legally changed. He thought it'd be great to be Elvis, sign his autographs at the various post offices, get Elvis stationary, an Elvis charge card, a driver's license, everything. The only trouble is that about two thousand other Elvis impersonators got the same idea. So there's more than two thousand legal Elvises travelling around the world. Don't forget, Japan holds its own annual Elvis impersonation convention every August and more that 100, 000 people show up, including no less that 500 Elvises appearing on stage.

Louis Krantz, aka Elvis takes out a Walkman and hands it to me. "Listen. Tell me what you think." I listen. Kid Elvis has recorded "Mystery Train", "Blue Moon", and "Trying To Get To You." The tape is about an hour long, but I listen to only those three cuts. The kid Elvis is good, which means he does sound like Elvis, even though the musicians behind him sound as though they'd rather he be playing Guns & Roses. Here's a horrible thought. Do you think that in twenty years from now there will be 30,000 Axl Rose imitators and an Axl Rose postage stamp?

I take the headphones off. Louis Krantz, aka Elvis is anxious to know what I think. "Kid Elvis," I say, "you do a good young Elvis. But," (and I don't want to hurt the kid's feelings but as I get older I find the truth takes a lot less time to get to than it used to) "I think you have a great voice, but maybe you should try to find your own style, your own songs."

Kid Elvis looks at me like I'm crazy. "This is my music, and this is my style. Don't you understand, I'm Elvis!"

I think to myself, "Hey, I'm too old for this. I'm sitting across from a kid who has bought into his own fantasy." I look into Kid Elvis's eyes. "No sale." "Gone for the weekend." "Nobody home."

"Well, you're right," I say. I've been in this situation before. What you've got to do is make quiet, polite conversation. Don't make any sudden moves. Smile. Agree. "What I meant is that even Elvis had to find himself. You know, early on he wanted to be another Dean Martin."

"I know exactly what you're saying," Kid Elvis says. "You're just like my father. Your whole generation should just die out, catch some disease and vanish."

"Don't worry," I say quietly, "we are." I reach for the check.

"Leave it there," Kid Elvis says, and he throws down a fifty dollar bill. The Postal Service must be paying really well.

I get up and wish the kid good luck. We know it isn't going to be easy, not with 30,000 Elvis impersonators fighting over the same dollar. And how many stamps can the Postal Service issue?

I tell the kid goodbye, but he's got his Walkman phones on, bouncing to the tape and can't hear me. By the tempo of his head bobs and leg twitches, my guess is that he's listening to "Baby, Let's Play House" or maybe "My Baby Left Me." In any case, I've got to find a different restaurant to hang out in, at least until all the United States Postal Service Elvis Impersonators have left Memphis. I mean, there's not even enough room in this town for one Elvis, not even the real one.

Twenty-Nine: Old Shep

After leaving Kid Elvis at Biggun's, I take a walk along Beale Street and end up in W. C. Handy Park, which has seen better days. I run into an old guy there. He must be in his eighties. I swear, every old person in Memphis has a story. His name is Elias Hammer. He tells me that he has lived in Memphis except for a time after the 1937 flood when his familiy's house was washed away down the Wolf River and into the Mississippi. He worked in Nashville for awhile and got to know a number of musicians, one who claimed he wrote "Old Shep". The old man said that his friend based the song on a series of stories that appeared in the papers in the late '30's.

Elias Hammer seemed to think that the incident occurred in a small town in Montana. A Sheepherder had died. They put him in a cheap pine coffin and took him down to the train station to ship him home. What nobody noticed was that his dog, a mangy German Shepherd, had followed the coffin to the station. Train stations were busy places back then, so the dog went unnoticed for days.

It's an impossible story to corroborate, but the dog would come up to every arriving train just to find his master. The telegraph operator was the first to notice the dog. And it was he who finally put the pieces together. The dog continued to try to find his master on every incoming train, because he knew he had left on one. This went on through the winter, and winters in Montana can be pretty mean. The shepherd just dug a hole under the station and waited for trains. Naturally, the telegraph operator saw that the dog was fed, and he told some operators in neighboring stations about the dog. They, in turn, passed the word along, until the story was picked in the national papers.

People wrote in that they'd adopt the dog, and some even showed up at the station, but the telegraph operator knew that the dog wanted to stay at the station to keep looking for his master. The dog was featured in Ripley's Believe It Or Not, and began to receive as many as a hundred letters a day from people across the country, sending money and offers to adopt the dog.

This went on for another six years. By this time the shepherd's senses were growing dim. One winter's day he was wandering in the yard and didn't hear or see the train as it pulled into the station. The dog was run over and died on the spot. More than a thousand people came to his funeral, which was featured in all the papers.

It was then that Elias Hammer's friend sat down and wrote "Old Shep" and showed it to some of the musicians he knew up in Nashville. Next thing he knew, a couple of those good ole boys had recorded the song and were making money. Elias's friend tried to talk to the publishers and at least two of the record companies that had issued his song, but they listened politely, thanked him for his time, and showed him the door. Of course, the composer of "Old Shep" could have hired a lawyer, if he could have afforded one, but the record companies have staffs of lawyers. Even if you're right, they can outspend you and break you. So, according to Elias Hammer, somebody else got credit for writing "Old Shep".

And what happened to the musician who wrote "Old Shep"? He kept working as a studio musician writing songs that never sold. The man finally packed it in, became an insurance salesman. His name has been forgotten, lost through the years, like him, an ambient refinement of dust.

Twenty-Nine: Old Shep

It's an old story. Until his dying day, Moon Milligan swore that Hank Williams stole "Jamabalaya" from him, Mississippi Fred McDowell said that Mick Jagger took credit for "You Gotta Move" and Jerry Lee lewis took credit for "The End of the Road" even though it was written by Irving Berlin and recorded by Frankie Laine years before Jerry Lee Lewis got bounced out of the Waxahachie Bible Institute.

Elias Hammer and I talk for awhile before I head back to the hotel. "That's all he wanted was what was his," Elais Hammer said. "One chance is all you need, and one chance is all you get, if that. Now if those people was honest...." Elias Hammer's voice trails off. Then he says, "What am I talking about? Those musicians are all hungry. I wouldn't give you five cents for any of them up in Nashville, which is why I come back to Memphis. Lots of musicians here. All broke except a few. But they're real. Not like in Nashville."

We say goodbye. Elais Hammer takes out a plastic bag filled with popcorn and throws it on the ground. About a dozen pigeons who have been disgracing the statue of W. C. Handy come sailing down. Elias Hammer, looks around, takes a cloth-covered pipe from under his coat, bludgeons one of the pigeons, picks it up and heads out of the park.

Thirty: Mysterious Blood & The New Cancer Cure

Things like this happen only in Memphis. First, there is the woman who was dying of cancer. The cancer was originally in her lungs, then it spread, first to her liver, her stomach and finally to her bones. Everything ached so much that she wasn't able to walk. She couldn't bear to be touched. She had gone from weighing a 157 pounds down to 96 pounds. Her doctors had tried everything, from radiation to chemotherapy, but nothing could reverse the onslaught of the disease as it devoured her body, cell by cell, ounce by ounce each day.

Simply put, the doctors had given up and suggested that the family get ready for the inevitable. The woman began to put things in order. She rewrote her will, bought a plot in the cemetery near her church, and began to write letters to her friends and relatives about her illness and that she wanted to thank them before she died for being in her life.

Then something extraordinary happened. After writing four letters the first day, the woman was exhausted. But the second day found her feeling stronger than she had felt in months. She completed twelve letters that day. While writing letters on the third day, the woman realized that she wasn't feeling as much pain as she usually did. By the fourth day, she had written twenty-four letters and felt so good that she got out of bed. For the first time in weeks she felt like getting out of her pajamas and into regular clothes and even having a meal at the kitchen table.

The fifth day was a Sunday, and she was feeling very strong. She decided that she wanted to go to church. After church services, she came home and had dinner with her family and ate everything that was served. However, she didn't write any letters that day, so on the sixth day, the woman began to feel weak again. She went back to bed late in the morning and slept all day. Her family gathered around her, sensing that the disease was only in brief remission and that death would finally have its way.

On the seventh day, she struggled out of bed and began to pay some of the bills that kept pouring in and sent all the forms to her health care provider, who us old folks used to call, Doctor. By nightfall, she was feeling better again.

Something in the dark recesses of her mind began to stir. She had begun to give careful attention to the subtle pattern of sickness and well-being. She noted that on the days that she wrote letters, she felt great. She became weakened when she stopped writing letters and paying bills. Based on this observation, the woman decided to write to everyone she could think of, whether she cared about them or not, each and every day. She even wrote her silent and secure representatives about Clinton's attempt to cut off cost-of-living increases to people receiving Social Security. She wrote Bill Clinton about his commitment to lowering the cost of health care. "Dear Mr. President, if you think the cost of living has gone up," she wrote, "try dying."

She grew stronger. All pain disappeared. She wrote more letters every day. Then suddenly, even though she continued to write letters, she began to weaken. She lay in bed trying to figure out what went wrong. Maybe she was only in remission, and now the disease was at full gallop, her body feeding each mutating cell, one at a time, into irreversible, self-devouring inner atrophy that plies its trade in the dark. She tried to go over everything. Had anything changed? She still used the same stationary. She still used Paper-mate Flexgrip pens, because the rubberized coating felt soft, yet firm in her hand.

Then one night, while she was floating in and out of consciousness, it came to her. She had changed one thing. In her zeal for writing, she had run out of Elvis stamps. Her granddaughter had gotten her new ones with flowers. The woman sat bolt upright in bed and yelled, "I need Elvis stamps." Her family came running in, thinking that this was the end, that delirium had set in, and next would be the coma, followed by death. But it wasn't delirium.

"Get me some Elvis stamps," she called out to them, as they gathered around her bed. "Now," she implored.

Her family stood around, gazing, agape and paralyzed. Was this the end? Should they humor her? Grant her her last wish, no matter how crazy? Of course. Always give the dying what they want. Her son had purchased eight sheets of Elvis stamps as an investment for his retirement. "I think I have some," he said, and left the bedroom to get them.

In a few minutes he returned with about eight stamps. No sense wasting a whole sheet on a babbling woman in the throes of death. The woman reached out greedily for the stamps. She took them and stuck out her dry, white, withered tongue and began to lick. "More stamps," she pleaded. Everyone looked at her son. "She needs more stamps," his sister shouted. With great reluctance, the son went back into his room and brought in the remaining thirty-two stamps from the dismembered, collectable sheet. The dying woman, somewhat revived, took the stamps from her son's hand. "Water," she said. "I can't lick these stamps without water. I'm too dry." Someone brought her a glass of water from the bathroom sink.

Within an hour, the woman was fully-conscious, and she got out of bed to watch Jay Leno, regretting that Johnny Carson had been replaced by a horseshoe jawed substitute who sounded like he was trying to sell a dilapidated used car, its transmission filled with sawdust, its crankcase awash in the thick, dark fluid of Bardahl End Smoke, everytime he told a joke.

Within days, the woman was out in the yard, thinking about planting a garden when spring came. Her doctor has submitted the woman to every known test and he couldn't explain the sudden, complete disappearance of the cancer. No growth on the kidney. No spot on the lung. Her merest symptom of any disorder is her light cough which her doctor attributes to a slight build-up of mucilage from licking too many Elvis stamps.

As soon as word got out, there was a run on Elvis stamps. People came to the Memphis main post office in motorized wheel chairs, on canes and crutches, aluminum walkers bearing portable oxygen tanks to buy Elvis stamps. "Lick the image of the King and you will be cured," cried out Reverend Elder Solomon Lightfoot Littlejohn from his pulpit in the Holy Host Temple of the Divide Spirit. Only in Memphis.

Now to the mysterious blood. What appeared to be blood has been dripping down the walls in a rooming house on Beale Street. That's where an elderly couple live. The wife is on a dialysis machine three days a week. One night the wife heard something dripping. She thought it was the faucet, but when she checked all the faucets, she found that the taps were shut tight and there was no sign of water dripping. The next night she heard the dripping again. Finally, by the fourth day, what appears to be blood started coming out of the living room wall and is forming the face of Elvis. She called the police right away. The police sent samples of the blood to the State Crime Lab, in Memphis. They verified that the substance was indeed water turned a reddish rust color from a leaky pipe somewhere on the second floor.

One policeman on the scene contacted the landlady. She lives directly above the wall with the face of Elvis. There is still the rumor that the water is really blood and that there is a police cover-up. When asked what the blood type was and if it happened to be the same type as Elvis's, the police spokeswoman, Jenifer Hammond, said, "The police are conducting a complete and thorough investigation and you can be certain that the final determination will conclude that there is a rational explanation for the reappearance of the stain. It will take time since this is an extremely rare situation."

Finally, a reporter from the *Commercial Appeal* got inside the room with the leaking face of Elvis. He talked the couple into letting him take some photographs of their wall. It turned out that the stain wasn't from a leaking pipe, but from a backed up down spout filled with dead leaves that has overflowed and seeped into their wall. And the face on the wall doesn't look like Elvis or like anyone. It looks more like a map of India or of Texas without that western droop of land below I-90. This is like those stories about people who see a vision of the Virgin Mary in the side of a gnarled maple or Jesus's face in a cloud formation.

Not that anyone knows what Mary or Jesus looked like. So, Jesus had long hair and a beard. That means that that cloud could either look like Jesus or maybe Don McLean and John Fogerty. Only in Memphis.

Thirty-One: Ghost On The Heating Grate

I call home to let my family know where I am, to find out how they are, and learn if there are any messages. The only messages are questions from readers who want to be included in the Pop Quizzes. My eight-year-old son wants to add a question to the quizzes. I tell him he can't. But he tells me he should be able to because I'm his dad and he has the right to quiz me. Are kids getting smarter earlier or am I slowing down? As John Cage used to say: "If you don't know, why do you ask?"

Pop Quiz Seven
    1. Elvis sang "Love Me Tender" in 1956. The song's original title was:
        1. "Aura Lee"
        2. "Annabelle Lee"
        3. "Walking With Mr. Lee"
        4. "Shirley & Lee"
        5. "Terry Lee"

    2. My son asks what was the name of Elvis's miniature horse? Was it:
        1. Mr. Ed
        2. Pony Boy
        3. Hound Dog
        4. Flaming Star
        5. Col. Thumb

3. In G.I. Blues, Elvis sings "Wooden Heart". Who had the best-selling single? Was it:
  1. Dicky Lee
  2. Bruce Channel
  3. Roger Miller
  4. Joe Dowell
  5. Charlie Rich

4. In Roustabout, Elvis sings "Little Egypt". Who had the original hit version of the song? Was it:
  1. The Searchers
  2. The Coasters
  3. The New Seekers
  4. Gene Pitney
  5. The Monkees

After calling home, I take a walk down Beale Street. The weather's turned cold, and it drizzled all night, so Memphis is veiled in a morning fog. I head toward Alfred's, hoping it's open this early. I have crossed Biggun's off my list, which is unfortunate, because it's one place I really enjoy.

As I walk up Beale Street, I think about spring and heading to Montana to do some fishing with some of the fishing buddies, like Gabe, the Nose, Dave Cigars, and Tony the Clam. I have also promised my son that I would take him to Disney World, and to Universal Studios when I get back home. I am thinking about the stalled negotiations with National Public Radio about doing a series on Old Radio Shows, when I literally walk into the ghost on the heating grate. He's there to keep warm, because as I metioned the weather has turned gray and raw. You've seen them in your own town. Old woven stained coat from the Salvation Army, the inside of the shoes lined with newspapers to fill the holes in his soles. The vinous, bloodshot eyes, the wild gray hair, that simultaneous look of fear and contempt that goes way back across generations, that goes way back from Chicago, from Memphis,

Thirty-One: Ghost On The Heating Grate

from the Mississippi Delta, to Tampa Red, to whoever it was who taught Robert Johnson how to play, way up in back country to whoever taught Ruby MCoy and Fred and Annie McDowell, far back somewhere deep from the Georgia Sea Islands, and all the centuries of pain and distrust all wrapped up into one soul. And this that man, wrapped in early Memphis morning fog, looks at me with generational ghost hatred, as though, even if he didn't have a home, didn't have a warm place other than that heating grate, and even if the next meal was a sure thing, he could at least hate someone who somewhere along the way might be related to the people who took his people from their homes across the ocean, how many generations ago?

And what should I do about it? Take him to breakfast at Alfred's, like it's national brotherhood week and get both of us kicked out? Do I hand him some money? Maybe drop some money on the ground? Give him the choice of picking it up or letting it blow away? As usual, I do nothing. I walk by him in the fog, nod in his direction and he nods back. We can either see each other as victims of something that started long ago or we can recognized that we're just visiting, our bones on loan and we don't know when the lease is up. I used to think that the next world will be better. That's what they told me in the last one.

Answers to Pop Quiz Number Six. "Aura Lee" is the original title of "Love Me Tender". It is the alma mater of West Point. I am relying on my son for the answer to the name of Elvis's miniature horse. He saw pictures of the horse on Nickelodeon while I was out of town. He says the horse's name was "Hound Dog."

I was hoping for Col. Thumb, but the real Colonel wouldn't allow that to happen. "Wooden Heart" was a hit for Joe Dowell, on Smash Records, which was also the label Charlie Rich, Roger Miller, Dicky Lee and Bruce Channel recorded for at various times in their career. Quickly now, who played harmonica on Bruce Channel's "Hey Baby"? No, it wasn't Stevie Wonder, Toots Thielemans (who plays harp on the theme from"Sesame

Street"), Larry Adler, Jerry Murad, Charley McCoy or Charlie Musselwhite, but it was Delbert McClinton, the world's last roadhouse maverick.

"Little Egypt" was first recorded by the Coasters. I include the Searchers, New Seekers, Gene Pitney, and The Monkees because they might have recorded "Little Egypt" , but who would ever know? Does anyone actually buy recordings by any one of the aforementioned artists? If so, please go to your music collections right now and delete these artists. If insanity is doing the same thing over and over and expecting different results, insanity is also listening to Gene Pitney and/or The Monkees and expecting them to one day sound good.

Anyway, I make to the restaurant. Alfred's is closed. I walk a few blocks toward the Peabody Hotel and walk into Joe's Diner. The heat feels good down to the bone, and the smells of home fries and bacon are rich and abundant.

I order ham and scrambled eggs. I do not order grits. This is the New South. A Yankee ordering grits when everyone knows how awful they taste is patronizing. I will gladly patronize anyone serving corn fritters or chicken and dumplings made from scratch, but I will not patronize anyone over something that should not be consumed, but used, if necessary, to cover the bottom of bird cages or hen houses or tossed under your spinning wheels to get you out of a snowbank.

Thirty-Two: El Vez at Bad Bob's

This is the winter of our disc content. RCA has opened the vaults and released everything they can find recorded by Elvis. Still not found are alternate versions of "Trying To Get To You" and other Sun recordings sold to RCA, then immediately lost. Of course, any real Elvis fan knows that the material went downhill as soon as Elvis signed up with His Master's Voice. I think the real difference is between the two cities where Elvis recorded. Memphis is the Home of the Blues, and Nashville, well Nashville is the Athens of the West, faux-cultured, fax littered, technically advanced, sterile, a town filled with musicians who can play anything behind anyone flawlessly with their eyes closed, and often do.

Maybe it was the addition of Floyd Cramer and Chet Atkins to the RCA sessions that ethnically cleansed the early RCA recordings. After that, it was the Ken Darby singers, and then the shift from music written by black writers to white song writers. "Surrender" was recorded before as "Return to Sorrento", and "It's Now or Never" was "O Solo Mio", a hit a decade earlier for Mario Lanza. The writing moved from Arthur "Big Boy" Crudup, Little Richard, Otis Blackwell, Roy Brown, Junior Parker, Ray Charles, and Jesse Stone to Teschmacher and DeCapua, Leibler and Stoller, Pomus and Schuman, Eddie Rabbit, and Mac Davis.

Like McDonald's, RCA can boast that more than a billion Elvis records sold, but like McDonald's, much of the Elvis RCA records had little taste, weren't lean, and seldom served piping hot. Dear folks at RCA: Please, no more repackaging. Send someone down to Nashville and dig through the warehouse to find those lost Sun Studio recordings. Give us something rare and well done.

In the meantime, one thing you can't escape in Memphis is the caravan of nomadic Elvis impersonators. Some of them are getting more inventive. A new Elvis to hit town also includes two sidemen who look exactly like Bill Black and Scotty Moore. They play nothing but early Elvis accoustically. They also play, "Tomorrow Night", a classic written by the great guitarist and singer, Lonnie Johnson, a song recently ruined by Bob Dylan. Why would anyone buy a Dylan nasal disc when the could buy the real thing? Try finding the Lonnie Johnson King recordings, or pick up Blues Boy BB300, which includes "In Love Again", a hit song waiting to happen.

Another innovative Elvis impersonator has put together the Million Dollar Quartet. There's a kid with wide ears and peroxide blond hair who can play the piano incredibly well. There is a young, pre-hairpiece, rocking guitar player who has mastered the licks of Carl Lee Perkins.

Also in the group a young, pre-Colonel Parker Elvis, who occasionally sits down at the piano to sing spirituals recorded by Elvis. His "Swing Down, Chariot" is especially moving. In fact, he is so good, it's too bad he's decided to be an Elvis impersonator, because he's one of the few who has a chance to develop on his own.

Of course, there is a fourth member of the group, a tall, black-haired guitarist with a deep voice. He's supposed to be Johnny Cash, the pre-benzedrine era. Together, the group leaves something to be desired. Except for the Johnny Cash impersonator, the musicians could make it on their own, but they don't play well together. This makes them all the more authentic, a small group with all those egos crashing. Jerry Lee Lewis did play back-up behind Carl Perkins and Johnny Cash, as, years later, Carl Perkins played behind Johnny Cash, but they could never work a unit. And as a member of the Million Dollar Quartet, the real Johnny Cash was at the original session for only a few minutes, just long enough to pose standing at the piano behind Elvis, Carl

Thirty-Two: El Vez at Bad Bob's

and Jerry Lee before he left the recording studio to go grocery shopping with his first wife, Vivian.

The most interesting Elvis impersonator in town is El Vez. I think he's Mexican. The first time I saw him, he was performing at Bad Bob's. Of course, no one mistakes him for Elvis. I mean, he's got the usual 1970's sequined Elvis jump suits and does a lot of Elvis's hits, but he can't pass for Elvis any more than Joni Mitchell could be mistaken for Aretha Franklin. And I've noticed one thing that all the Elvis impersonators have in common. While they're on stage, and after they get off stage, they all think that they are actually Elvis incarnate. It's a strange phenomenon to watch. I'll talk to the impersonators before they get their Elvis costumes on, and they're insurance salesmen, car dealers, washing machine repairmen, mailmen, short order cooks and unemployed aircraft workers. But as soon as they jump into their jumpsuits, stand back. It's like the Elvis incubus has jumped inside with them and has taken over their minds and bodies. You can't talk to these guys anymore. Their voices get lower, they rock their shoulders, and swing their heads. A few seem to put on weight as you are talking to them. Their knees develop discernable twitches, and suddenly you find yourself in a room where a working stiff is transformed before you eyes from Jekyll to Hyde, possessed, ready to go on stage and sing the Devil's music.

An hour later, they come off stage, still possessed, sweaty, eyes glazed, talking so deeply that it comes out as one, long, slurred, mumbled word. And it isn't until hours later that you see the Elvis impersonator as he was before he was transformed by a greater power. They tend to hang around back stage long after their performance is over and the lights are being turned off. They seem to be shorter than you remember. Not as lean and mean. Their voices are high and there is no fire in their eyes. No power in his hand shake. No matter what you ask them, what seems to come back is, "Hello, my name is Jeffrey. I'll be your server tonight. What size fries do you want? What can I do to get you into this baby today? I'm sorry, but it looks like I'm going to have to take the wahing machine back to the shop.

I follow one of the Elvis imitators to the parking lot. His body seems rigid, as he carries his imitation 1970's Elvis jumpsuit in a semi-clear plastic garment bag over his right shoulder as he heads for his 1978 Bonneville. Where does he go next? To Chicago? Philly? Dallas? To Little Rock? No. Has his has left a message to head over to the Eddie Rice Funeral Escort Service. The car they just leased has a stuck accelerator; the washing machine won't drain; the telephone let's you call out but no one can call in.

The Elvis impersonator lays his genuine replica jump suit delicately, lovingly, across the back seat. He gets into the driver's seat, scans the desolate parking lot. Where are the crowds, the adulation, the screaming Elvis fans he heard just an hour ago? He picks up the clip board and the Arrow Guide from the passenger's seat. He checks out the address of the Eddie Rice Funeral Escort Service. He starts his Bonneville up. There is a roar and the usual blue smoke of burning oil curling out of the blackened tail pipe. He thinks that just as soon as he makes it, he's going to get the muffler fixed and the valves ground. But for now, baby, he just hopes he's got the parts to fix the accelerator, a plumber's snake long enough to unclog the bathtub drain, and the right schematic to make the right connections so the newly-bereaved can call in for escort service. Because, right now, times are tough in Memphis. Unless you've won the lottery or you see Ed McMahon walking up to your doorwith an oversized check, this is not time to give up your day job, if you have one.

Thirty-Three: The Opened Grave

Security at Graceland isn't what it used to be when Elvis lived there when there was always the possibility of Jerry Lee Lewis driving up at two in the morning, waving a gun, climbing onto the gates and demanding to see the King. Early on the security force was made up of family members who needed work, trusted friends, hangeres on and friends of hangers on, the family connections growing more remote through the years as uncles and cousins died off. Now the security guards are outsiders and, for the most part, could be working at Burger King. To them, it's just a job.

All Memphis is abuzz with the word that some people had dug up Elvis's grave during the night. Instead of leaving at closing time, they hid on the grounds until dark. Their motives aren't clear, but digging up the bodies of stars isn't anything new. When Charlie Chaplin died in Lausanne, Switzerland, on Christmas Day in 1977, two vandals exhumed his cadaver in March later and heldthe great comedian's body hostage for a million dollars. The plot was unsuccessful. Charlie Chaplin's body was found buried in a field about a mile from his estate, in Lausanne. Roman Wardas, the leader of the theft, went to prison for nearly five years. His partner, Gantscho Ganev, considered of limited intelligence, was given a suspended sentence. Since then, Charlie Chaplin's body has been buried in a lead vault with an intricate alarm system to prevent another thief attempt.

At Graceland, the vandals started digging after midnight and finally raised the heavy coffin liner around four a.m. They hadn't taken into account that the liner would be bolted shut, so they failed to bring any tools with them except shovels. They were so intent to get the body that they began to try to pry the liner off with the thick blades of their shovels. When this didn't work, they began to slam the bolts with their shovels. The ringing of metal on metal coming from the Meditation Garden awakenedlerted thethe well-trained and alert security guards who immediately called in the Memphis police. By the time the police arrived, the marauders had succeeded in wresting the liner lid from the rusted bolts. The coffin was on the ground, tilted on its side, the marble grave cover with the bronze plaque written by Vernon, was on top of Vernon's grave. When the police shined their flashlights into Elvis's coffin, it was empty.

A search of the grounds of Graceland found the four would-be thieves hiding in of the empty stables. The police wanted to know what the theives, three men and one woman, had done with Elvis's body. They looked stunned. They said that when they opened the coffin, not two minutes before the police arrived, they found the coffin just as it is. Empty.

Of course, the police didn't believe the witless intruders. They immediately called for more police to cordon off the streets surrounding Graceland. Names were taken, the vandals were searched and their identification cards were taken and radioed in to check for outstanding warrants and previous arrests.

By six o'clock, it started to get light. It had been raining the day before, so the ground around the Meditation Garden was soft. The gang of four showed two Memphis plain-clothesmen where they hid before closing time. It was clear that several sets of footprints led from behind some bushes to the gravesite of Elvis. At that point, the ground is trampled by hundreds of footprints where the vandals struggled to dig up the coffin and wrestled the liner lid off. You can see the sets of footprints coming from the front of Graceland to the grave of Elvis where the police interrupted the vandals from their work. But it is also clear that there are no footprints leading away from the grave

Thirty-Three: The Opened Grave

in any direction. Unless the vandals had an accomplice who used a helicopter, could teleport himself or used some other form out out-of-body travel, there is no way anyone could have made off with a body.

What has happened is clear. Someone or some group has made off with the body that was contained in the fake Elvis grave. Someone has made off with Jimmy Hoffa's body, mistaking it for Elvis's. But who would want to do that? As disturbing as this might be, the fact that Hoffa's body was stolen gives credence to something that Greil Marcus writes about in his book, DEAD ELVIS. What he says is not easy to take, so if you are easily offended by cannibalism, I suggest that you don't read any further. Go directly to Chapter Thirty-Four.

When I read the following passages, I found the imformation they contained hard to believe. I'm only paraphrasing here because I don't have the Greil Marcus book with me. In DEAD ELVIS, Greil Marcus reports that some people had dug up Elvis's body and sold it to some entrepreneurs, in Europe. Once again, I mention that this is third-hand information and I might not have my information dead solid perfect, so I suggest that you read Greil Marcus's book for all the details.

However, in summary, those remarkable European entrepreneurs had Elvis's body ground up and were selling Elvis burgers for $1,000 each. It was rumored that Mick Jagger bought one. I I'm sorry to report that I didn't ready beyond that point.

Here is something that those European entrepreneurs overlooked. When Elvis faked his death, it was Jimmy Hoffa's body that was placed in Elvis's casket. So, if Mick found the burger a little tough, grisly and on the fatty side now he knows why.

The people at Graceland don't want the current attempt at grave robbing reported, because it reveals that there was a previous, successful one. Even with Elvis really leaving the building, the management team at Graceland has enormous power. They bring in millions of dollars in tourism to the Memphis economy every year. Any hint of a scandal could ruin the operation. But knowing what ghouls might are walking around in AmericaMemphis, even more people might come to see the grave from where the (not real) body of Elvis was stolen.

The Memphis police will write up their reports that four trespassers were sighted and apprehended, and released. No names, please. The four grave robbers are given the option of getting their asses kicked by the police or getting out of town. The vandals gratefully accept the latter offer after one of them is cracked in the ribs with a rubberized "convincer."

The Memphis *Press-Scimitar* is called in. They will write a nice article about the alert security police at Graceland apprehending four devoted Elvis fans who couldn't bear to leave the home of the King, had forgotten what time it was, and were accidentally locked inside Graceland. If you have read the Warren Report: The Official Report on the Assassination of President John F. Kennedy, you know how these things are handled.

Okay, you ask. What about the four grave robbers? Won't they tell what they found? But who will believe them? Do you think that the New York *Times* or the Chicago *Tribune* will take them seriously? What you might find someday is an article in the National *Enquirer* or The World Weekly *News*. You know the articles I mean: "Wax JFK Found In Coffin," "Amelia Earhart Found In Samoa", "Elvis Sighted At Washington Jack In The Box." You know, stuff so true that we could never believe it.

Thirty-Four: Them Changes

Like most people, I am a creature of habit, especially when I'm on the road. When I come to Memphis, I always stay at The Peabody, on Beale Street, but I never order roast duck. I'll wander into Lansky's not because I want to buy anything, but because they always have men's clothing in colors that you'll see six months later in L. A. I used to stop in at Sun Studios when it was called Memphis Recording Service, but now I don't walk by it. There used to be a coffee shop next door, around the corner. When I rent a car it's still from Avis, even though Enterprise and even Rent-A-Wreck have moved to Memphis.

Some of the old restaurants have disappeared, and I notice that hundreds of Chinese and Indian restaurants have sprung up since I last lived here, in 1962. What was I doing in Memphis, in 1962? Studio musician at the new Sam Phillips Recording Service at 639 Madison Avenue. I came to Memphis because of the music. By the time I got here everyone who had made the music I dug was gone. Carl Lee Perkins and John R. Cash were with Columbia. Jerry Lee Lewis was still cutting a few sides, but he had begun spiraling down that slippery slope of anger and pain to care about music just then. He still was under contract with Sun Records, but after the marriage scandal and getting banned from most rock radio stations, Jerry set foot in a studio. It took the effect of several of his friends to encourage Jerry to get back in the studio. Sam Phillips had built a new recording complex at 639 Madison Avenue, not far from the origoinal Sun recording studio.

When Jerry got back in the studio, he recorded a fine vesion of Ray Charles' "What'd I Say." In a few weeks Jerry was back on the charts and England called, then all of Europe, for Jerry to come on tour because everything had been forgotten.

It seemed to me that the only one happening was Charlie Rich, on the Sun Subsidiary label, Phillips International. He was the only one who was still hungry enough to cut good records. David Houston had a brief shot and Billy Adam's "Reconsider Baby" could have made it, but the energy to promote just wasn't there. Those three by two inch ads in Cashbox just didn't have the sway they once had.

My unofficial connection with Sun Records goes back before 1962 forward. When Jerry Lee Lewis's records were banned from the air, I used to buy my records from Tom Phillip's Select-O-Hits, on Chelsea Avenue and hand carry them to radio stations and record stores.

I used to carry those records into major cities where I was playing with my band, The Bluesberries. I remember visiting Alan Freed one night in New York. I'm fairly certain that it was in 1958 and that he was at WINS. Nobody but nobody was playing any Jerry Lee Lewis, even though he had released a killer first class record called "Lovin' Up A Storm". Forget that Jerry Lee had married his 13-year-old cousin. Just the titles of his records could get him banned from radio play. Come to think of it, this could have been early 1959. Jerry Lee had released two quiet songs after his marriage was revealed, "Break-Up" and "I'll Sail My Ship Alone". "Lovin' Up A Storm" was the return to full power.

Alan Freed had this screening process. You couldn't get in to see him unless he knew someone you knew who he could trust. The Feds had been putting the squeeze on him for payola so he had become a cautious man. I am not sure why I was let in. I just showed copies of Jerry Lee's record and explained why I was there.

Not only did I get into the radio station, but a woman named Peggy ushered me into the studio as soon as the ON AIR sign went off. Once I got into the studio, Alan glanced in my direction, nodded, but kept banging loudly on the console with the pot open while he played "I'll Be Satisfied" by Jackie Wilson. Not content to play it over once, Alan Freed, the allege radio father of Rock & Roll, the second coming of Moondog, kept replaying the Jackie Wilson's "I'll BeSatisfied for a half hour, pounding along with his studio mike on so his rhythmic pounding could go over the air.

During a break, we said "Hi"; I told him why I was there. He said he had gotten a copy of "Lovin' Up A Storm" but hadn't played it yet. He took Jackie Wilson's purple-colored Brunswick record off the second turn table and replaced it with the bright yellow labeled Sun record. And when Alan Freed came back on the air, he played the living hell out of that record. He pounded the console as Jerry Lee raged and howled through aproximately a minute and forty two seconds of rock and roll ecstasy. Alan Freed had both turn tables alternately cued up, so the split second that one record came to an end, another one started up. And that's how it was that one night. Nothing but Jackie Wilson and Lerry Lee Lewis sailing across the wavering airwaves, from Manhattan to Philly, and if the night air carried it just right, the music careened west across to the lakefront of Chicago and breezed down south into the hils of Tennessee and beyond to every radio tuned to 1010 WINS fading in and out like a breathing thing from a canyoned walls of Manhattan.

Looking back, that just might have been one of the last great nights of rock'n'roll on radio. Soon after Buddy Holly, Richie Valens and J.P. Richardson nose dived into a snowbanked field, in Clear Lake, Iowa, Alan Freed was off the air because of a Federal Investigation on Payola, and the only place you could get rock'n'roll regularly was on American Bandstand, that trotted out such greasy prettyboys as Paul Anka, Bobby Rydell, Frankie Avalon, Fabian Forte, Freddie Cannon, and Chubby Checker. And it was right then, you knew that nothing, not that dry hump in the back seat, those long rides down rain slicked roads, and staying up just to make sure that the sun was going to rise, that nothing would ever be the same again.

So, that's why I came to Memphis. Got an agent who booked The Bluesberies in a tour with Ben E. King, Betty Everett and The Mighty Sparrow through the West Indies, then to Miami to the Deauville. We got in just after a hurricane had washed through the lobby. A huge crystal chandelier lay crushed and fragmented under its own weight on the tiled lobby floor. I checked the large announcement board too see what conventions were meeting at the Deauville. There were two. The Retired Naval Reserve and a National Shoe Convention. That first night on stage was harder than a hooker trying to stay monagamous.

Did I dump my agent? I tried to, but he had a contract, so I changed my name and the name of my band. It didn't matter. We became like thousands of other rock 'n' roll dreamers who had made the pilgrimage to Memphis to become famous. If we were lucky, we got a session to play or sing behind someone who was going to become famous but never quite reached the tipping point and made it. We became understudies to understudies who, if they were lucky, cut a record, posed with Elvis in a photo, returned home, got married, had kids, and on rare occasions when the decibel level would lower enough, they would look out the window, hear a train whistle in the night and think about that other life.

So, now I'm back in Memphis, staying at The Peabody, as I usually do. Why am I here? Just to visit the ghosts of my youth. To see if I can pick up some of the records I lost along the way. Walk the streets of my favorite haunts now gone to urban renewal. To turn slowly and take a long look at what Memphis has become, and then say goodbye, because what I imagined was still here has been gone a long time.

Thirty-Five: Elvis Saves, Elvis Delivers, and Elvis's Prodigy Progeny

Three articles have appeared about Elvis in the past week. Two days ago Elvis saved two children when they fell through the ice, in Schenectady, New York. The two boys, ages nine and seven, had gone out on the ice to visit their grandfather who was ice fishing at the time. Authorities said that the daytime temperatures had been fluctuating a great deal during the past week, at times reaching 48 degrees before falling below freezing each night.

Over a period of time this variation in temperature thinned the ice to the point of becoming hazardous. The grandfather had ignored the red flags placed along the bank and across parts of the frozen channel. "He evidently knew where to walk, or he was just plain lucky," Captain Mason, of the Schenectady Police said, "but his grandchildren were less lucky." Even though the grandsons weighed significantly less than their grandfather, they hit a thin spot in the ice and fell through.

When they fell through, they started screaming, as did several witnesses. The grandfather tried to reach them, but he, too, fell through the ice. One neighbor ran home to call police while another tried to pullhoist a fallen dead branch across the ice to the two boys who struggled not to fall permanently beneath the ice.

The water temperature was estimated at about 40 degrees, and any prolonged submersion in the channel could be fatal, especially to the grandfather who had recently recovered from by-pass surgery.

A man, about six feet tall, with dark features, appeared and walked out on the ice. By now a crowd had gathered and they began to shout at the man not to go out because he would more certainly fall through the ice. But the man kept walking and for some reason the ice held under his imposing size. He reached down and pulled the two children from the dark, icy current, then pulled their grandfather out. Witnesses could offer no reason why the ice where the children and grandfather had fallen did not cave in under the weight of four persons standing so near the edge of the broken ice after being rescued.

By then, members of Schenectedy's Police and Fire & Rescue Squads arrived on the scene. They immediately formed a human life-line to the channel by linking arms. As soon as they were handed each child, members of the Fire and Rescue Squad carried them up the slight embankment into their vehicles to get the children warm and to perform mouth-to-mouth resuscitation, if it was necessary. The grandfather was unconscious, so a gurney was handed down along the human chain of rescuers. The children were treated for exposure, but didn't require further care. The grandfather was taken to the Medical Center as a precautionary measure.

After the confusion had died down, witnesses gave accounts of the near-tragedy to police and to reporters. They all mentioned the man who walked out on the ice, that somehow miraculously wavered, but never cracked. In the rush of activity that occurred during and just after the rescue, they each described the man who walked on thin ice and came to the same conclusion. The man looked an awful lot like Elvis.

Yesterday, in Spokane, Washington, a woman and her husband were rushing to the hospital because she was in labor. The couple, recent arrivals from Nepal, ran a red light and were involved in a minor accident. The husband, Gonsar Tulku, ran toward the vehicle he had just struck, waving his arms and talking in a combination of Tibetan Nepalese and English. The other driver, not understanding what Mr. Tulku was saying, feared that Mr. Tulku

Thirty-Five. Elvis Saves, Elvis Delivers

was about to attack him. He put his car in reverse, stepped on the gas up and rapidly, rammed the car behind him speeding off. Witnesses at the scene of the accident jotted down the license number of the car as it sped away. However, Mr. Tulku began running toward the small crowd that had gathered. Fearing that they, too, were in danger of being attacked, a number of them ran from the intersection.

In the meantime, moans and cries could be heard coming from the Tulku's car. At first, a number of people at the scene thought that Mrs. Tulku had been injured during the accident. A tall man in the crowd came forward and addressed Mr. Tulku in a foreign language, perhaps NepaleseTibetan. This seemed to calm Mr. Tulku, and he and the stranger then approached Mr. Tulku's car. In a few minutes police arrived, but all they could do was witness the birth of Mr. and Mrs. Tulku's daughter, Tara. The infant and Mrs. Tulku were taken to Spokane General Hospital in an ambulance. Mr. Tulku was issued a summons for failure to obey a traffic signal and was then released. Mother, father, and daughter at last report are doing fine.

Once again, witnesses at the scene claim that the man who assisted in the birth, well, they couldn't be sure, but he did look an awful lot like Elvis.

Of course, it is unlikely that Elvis would be travelling across the country, from Schenectady to Spokane, in a day and happen upon the scene of two near-disasters. My guess is that there are an awful lot of people who look like Elvis. There are thirty thousand registered Elvis impersonators in the world. I've only heard of only one guy who looks like Pope John Paul, and two who look like Bill Clinton.

Perhaps what is occurring is a subtle form of mass-hysteria. People keep reading about Elvis sightings, and in a crisis, some emotional situation where the adrenalin flows, people imagine they see Elvis. If there are thirty thousand registered Elvises in the world, who is to say that there aren't another hundred thousand unregistered Elvis lookalikes?

Now, for the third article in the paper. A woman from Shreveport, Louisiana, claims that she was Elvis's lover. This woman is not to be confused with the woman who wrote about having Elvis's daughter in ARE YOU LONESOME TONIGHT. This woman, Chris Takahashi, claims that her son, Miles, now seventeen, is the result of an ongoing love affair that started during the filming of "It Happened At The World's Fair," where she worked as an extra. Ms. Takahashi, who has never married, has written the Presley Estate executors to request financial support to put her son through college. Ms. Takahashi has supplied photocopies of documents to support her claim, but officials in charge of Graceland say that they receive similar requests almost every week from women who claim that Elvis fathered their children.

What makes Ms. Takahashi's story unique is that her son started to play musical instruments when he was twenty months old. At three-years-old, he could read and comprehend the subtleties of major literary classics, and he displayed a preference for the works of Mark Twain, especially THE MYSTERIOUS STRANGER. In the third grade, Miles could beat every area advanced chess player, and at age eleven, he completed a perfect score in math on the Scholastic Aptitude Test, which is used at most major colleges as the conclusive entrance exam.

Ms. Takahashi has struggled to keep Miles's life as normal as possible, but he has often completed a year of high school assignments in a week. As a single parent, Ms. Takahashi found it difficult to balance time with her son. While she worked, he would write a sonata to amuse himself. He can master any Sega Genesis or Super Nintendo game within an hour, completing all the levels unscathed.

Miles Takahashi has suggested improvements to games to both NES and Sega. He has developed software that he hopes will eventually be purchased by the various game companies once they upgrade their systems.

Ms. Takahashi had hoped that she could avoid going to court to settle her claim with the Presley estate. She has not received any

Thirty-Five. Elvis Saves, Elvis Delivers

response from Graceland. With the use of photos, blood samples, genetic mapping and experts in the field of gifted children who will testify that heredity plays a huge role in developing prodigies, along with a small army of vicious southern attorneys, she is prepared to present her case.

Ms. Takahashi has statements from various scholars and geneticists to support her claim. Essentially, they will say that heredity, in harmony with culture and nature, produce the prodigy, that it is impossible to guess who or what will produce the exceptionally gifted child. The word they use is "synchrony," which means that when the various influences work in harmony, you very likely might end up with a prodigy.

To support Ms. Takahashi's claim, she contends that she has personal effects to prove her relationship with Elvis. She has hair that she cut from Elvis herself, articles of clothing he wore, still unwashed. She claims she has dozens of photos of Elvis, dressed and undressed. She has photos of the two of them performing various sexual acts, including intercourse. She even says that she has several vials of Elvis's semen frozen in a secret location.

Even if any orall ofthis is true, Ms. Takahashi will still have to prove that Miles is Elvis's son. After speaking to her at length, I wish her well. Of course, if it were only the issue of paying for college, it would be nothing. The Elvis estate, if you recall, brings in more than a billion dollars a year. Maybe the executors would be wise to pay for Miles's college with no questions asked. With Miles's abilities, he could get a scholarship anywhere. Let's face it. Bill Clinton got a scholarship to Oxford and I doubt if he could beat Ross Perot at checkers.

The big deal here is the estate. If the power brokers give Miles a dime, even if they flinch for a second, they could open up a potentially larger claim to a portion of the estate. If there is even a hint of validity to Ms. Takahashi's claim, she will be visited, she will be made an offer if she releases, in writing, all claims and rights, and agrees not to bring any litigation against the Godhead, known as Graceland.

And once this is done, Ms. Takahashi will not be allowed to speak of Elvis again. In return for any payment, she will submit all photos and negatives, all personal possessions and objects, all frozen vials. Everything. She will sign her name to the contract, giving her word that everything she has relating to Elvis has been willingly submitted to the Estate for no future considerations.

Of course, the one possession she would like to submit to the Estate, is the one possessions the Estate will deny exists. The future integrity of the Estate depends on it. As far as the Estate is concerned, Miles's father was just another Elvis impersonator.

Thirty-Six: The Last Riders Of The Purple Sage

It's late in the afternoon and I decide to head over to Fat Jacque's for some blackened red snapper. No sooner do I place my order when Red Stuckey comes over. Red Stuckey is a fiddle player from ages ago. He used to play with several Western Swing bands, and played with Hal "Lone" Pine's great group, the Riders of the Purple Sage. They were rivaled only by The Sons of The Pioneers, which at various times had Roy Rogers, The Farr Brothers, Pat Brady, Tim Spencer and Bob Nolan as its members. As a matter of fact, having Bob Nolan and Tim Spencer, the two great writers of cowboy songs, like "Cool Water" and "Tumbling Tumbleweeds", made all the difference.

Red Stuckey says he still plays when he gets the chance, like two weekends ago at Dollywood, even though he's probably in his late seventies or early eighties. He never had the ability of Johnny Gimble or the showmanship of Bob Wills, but he made a living doing what he liked, and how many of us can say that?

There is an uncanny ability that made Red famous. He was a professional freeloader. You know that old hunting adage: When a hickory nut falls in the woods, a deer will hear it, a bear will smell it, and an hawk will see it. And if someone has just ordered food, Red Stuckey will show up. and just as the bill arrives, Red will suddenly be called away on business.

Red will be welcomed company, so I invite him to join me, which he accepts with a semi-toothless grin behind his whiskered face. Red wants to know why I'm here. I tell him I'm doing some writing. He says that he's glad I gave up music, because he says it's a bad business now. 'You gotta produce or they throw you out. Look what Columbia Records did to Johnny Cash and RCA did to Hank Snow," Red says., "canned their asses." They sell millions of records for those companies, then they get old and they throw them out.

"There was a time when I was in the studio every day and even some nights," Red laughs, "but I haven't been inside a studio now for nearly twenty years. Recorded some Purple Sage songs for a budget company in the Sixties. I think they was called Tops Records. And that was that. Since then just studio gigs. Playing "Orange Blossom Special" and "Sweetheart, You Done Me Wrong", which I could play backwards in my sleep. And I got to go to Nashville to play. That's where all the money and action is. I'm living in the wrong place, as usual. But that's all right. I had my time. I'm out of it. I just don't get what's going on. Musicians with no edge to them. And listen to what they call country music on the radio now. All these pretty boys. Not a cowboy in the mix. Not one I bet who ever picked cotton, or by the looks of them, did a day of real work in their lives. They wear western hats and not a trace of sweat on it, they wear work shirts on stage and, like I said, they wouldn't know work if it pissed on their boot. And their puking, pussy, tame, middle of the road flat out, dull, two chord, music. Don't nobody do any real living anymore? Goddamn pansies in tight pants. Why, I'm willing to bet you....." Red's voice trails off as the waiter brings our drinks.

Red is having bourbon. I'm sipping a little Southern Comfort. I figure with Red settling in, I'm here for awhile. Meanwhile, to show his appreciation, Red continues to talk about his music career. He says that one time he was offered a chance to sign up with the Sons of the Pioneers after Hugh and Karl Farr left. But they were with RCA at the time, after moving from Columbia to Decca. "And, there was no way," Red said between sips of bourbon, "that you could get me or any sane person to sign with RCA. Everyone knew that it was a cursed label. Look at Caruso. He recorded for RCA when it was Victor Records, and he died young. Then you

Thirty-Six: The Last Riders Of The Purple Sage

got Glenn Miller. He disappears over the English Channel and they never find him. I think of that guy, Russ Columbo, you know, the guy who sang like Bing Crosby and killed himself back stage. He recorded for RCA. Then there was that Italian guy who sang "Be My Love" and other stuff. Mario Lanza. He's making a mint, then he's dead before he's forty. Around that same time, RCA has this black guy, nice voice. Has a hit record of "Goodnight My Love". Bevlin or Belvin. I think it was Jesse Belvin. Somebody slashes his tires in a club parking lot, and he drives out after a gig, maybe a little drunk. He crashes his car and he's dead.

"Then there's Jim Reeves. No better country singer than him. Million sellers. Then bang. He's dead. Car accident or plane crash. I can't remember anymore. I always get his death mixed up with Patsy Cline. Then there was Sam Cooke, who made a mess out of "Tennessee Waltz" . "Tennessee Waltz" is supposed to be just that. Slow. So he jazzes it up and sells a million copies. But what good does it do him? He's recording for RCA, so he gets shot in some L. A. motel, trying to attack some woman. Dead. I don't think he was thirty-years-old when he got it.

"He was thirty-three," I interrupt, as the waiter brings our red snappers...

"So, what's thirty-three," Red says. "When I was thirty-three..." Jesus, I can't remember anything from when I was thirty-three."

Red is silent for a few minutes while he digs into his red snapper, which, even by America's greatest chef, Paul Prudhommes's standards, is violently hot. But it tastes so good, that it's impossible to stop eating, at least for me. But Red feels he's got to finish his line of thinking because at his age he's never sure when he'll forget what he started to say.

"Where was I?" he asks. "Sam Cooke," I say. "Oh, yeah. I disremembered there for a second. Why would he want to ruin "Tennessee Waltz" I'll never know. You know Roy Orbison and Roger Miller recorded for RCA. Young guys and they're dead. And then you got Elvis. Making all that money and dying young.

All recorded for RCA, which is why I never signed on with The Sons of the Pioneers. I could have been rich and dead just like the rest of them poor bastards."

"What makes you so sure that Elvis is dead?" I ask, the Southern Comfort making me feel too comfortable.

"Is Elvis dead?" Red asks, taking huge bites of his red snapper without missing a beat in his conversation." "Don't tell me you're one of them people. He's dead all right. From the outside, Memphis looks like a big city, but when you've lived here as long as I have, you know that Memphis is a small town to us insiders. When something happens, we know about it. And believe me, when Elvis kicked off, that wasn't just local insider news, that was an earthquake. Elvis meant money. With him dead, the Chamber of Commerce and all the city fathers were shook. Believe me. They thought it was over. They didn't realize that a dead Elvis was worth more to them than the fat, live one. They didn't figure on all these tourists filling up the motels, and coming here to make Graceland a national shrine.

"Nobody comes here to remember that Martin Luther King died here, too. Ain't no one going to name a boulevard after him. And you know why? Because Martin Luther King never did and never will bring money to Memphis. You want a street named after you, you gotta somehow put money in some politicians' pockets.

"Is Elvis dead?" Red says, then draining his bourbon and signaling for another. "Let me tell you something. You know what they sell here? For a hundred dollars you can buy a film of Elvis's autopsy. Is that sick, or what? You can buy a little clear bottle with a strand of his hair inside sold by his barber. You can buy a piece of soap someone stole from Graceland. Is Elvis dead? Duke, they don't come and deader."

"Red," I say, "supposing I tell you that I've seen Elvis?"

"Well," Red says, "what's that supposed to prove? Son, every som bitch and his Aunt Tillie has seen Elvis. That don't prove nothing."

Thirty-Six: The Last Riders Of The Purple Sage

"What makes you so positive?" I ask.

"Don't you hear nothing?" Red says. "I already proved it to you. He's gotta be dead. He recorded for RCA, didn't he? So, that's that."

"Okay, Red, I guess you've made your point."

We finish out meal in relative silence. Just small talk about who is still alive and who isn't. Red tells me he ran into Carl Perkins about a week ago. Carl lives in Jackson, which is maybe sixty northeast of Memphis, off route 40, where he opened a restaurant called the Blue Suede Diner, or something like that. Old Carly is still on the wagon, which is okay if you have to, but Red wishes Carl would get rid of his assortment of curly toupees. Red says, "I told Carl, 'whatdya want to wear them things for? Your hair was never curly. Them rugs look a crazed steelwool.' Carl says. 'I want to look good,' and I tell him he'll never look good. Even with Elvis in the ground all these years, Elvis still looks better than you. I laugh like hell, but Carl, he doesn't laugh, only looks as me with a bemused shit eatin grin on his craggy face."

Once Red Stuckey gets hold of a subject he can't let go, especially when a waiter brings the check. Red figures if he keeps talking, he can pretend he didn't see the waiter drop the leather folder with the bill sticking halfway out. "That Carl, he's living in a nice ranch house on Country Club Lane. All his song writing royalties have kicked in, so he's doing all right. But he's still grousing about Sam Phillips and all the money he owes Carl, and I tell Carl, 'All you boys, Jerry Lee, John R., and you ought to get down on your knees every day and be thankful because without Sam, all you hillbillies would be walking behind a jackass plowing up some field. Carl still doesn't laugh, but I bet he knows it's true."

I pick up the check.

"You gonna be in town long?" Red asks.

"Could be, Red. I don't know just yet."

"You staying at the usual place?"

I nod, yes.

"Good," he says. "Maybe I'll give you a call." With that, Red Stuckey slides away from the table, thanks me for the dinner, then we wave so long to each other.

It's gotten chilly again. I pull my coat collar around my neck and head for my rented car and then the Peabody. Driving through Memphis late night traffic, I think about Red and his theory about RCA. Other artists who recorded for other labels died young. How about Charlie Parker, Robert Johnson, Bessie Smith, Johnny Ace, Frankie Lymon, and Little Willie John, to mention a few? But Red's theory is still remarkable. Who would have put all that history together about RCA, then refuse to sign a contract?

It's too bad. You know what's too bad? It's too bad that Yoko Ono never signed with RCA.

Thirty-Seven: Dirt Road Blues

Pop Quiz Number Eight.

1. Everyone knows that Highway 51 has been renamed Elvis Presley Boulevard. What other recording artist, movie actor and tv star has another Memphis boulevard named after him? Is it:
   1. Louis Armstrong
   2. Amos Jacobs
   3. John R. Cash
   4. Roy Acuff
   5. Memphis Minnie (Minnie McCoy)
   6. Memphis Slim (Peter Chatman, Sam Chatman's step-nephew)

It's too nice a day to hang around the Peabody, so I drive the eighty miles southeast to Tupelo. I haven't been there since Elvis's faked death, and I want to see what they've done to the town to cash in on the memory of the King. When Elvis was growing up, the town fathers were constantly chasing Vernon down for stealing wood and equipment from the Leake & Goodlett lumber yard where he worked before World War II. Supposedly, Vernon also kited checks, but it's difficult to imagine Vernon having a checking account, since he was often living of welfare. And, of course,

Elvis was an oddball looking freak who grew up feeling guilty for the stillborn death of his brother, Jesse. Imagine Elvis singing "Old Shep" in front of his fifth grade class, the same kids who used to chase him down and beat him up. What a tough, frightening childhood. Poverty surrounded by poverty. One book I haven't seen yet about Elvis is TUPELO MEMORIES: The People of Tupelo Who Knew Him Remember Elvis. His teachers tell how he daydreamed looking out the window while they tried to explain math. "If it takes one man six days to build a cabin, and it takes six men one day to build a cabin, and it takes one ship six days to cross the Atlantic, how many days will it take six ships to cross the Atlantic?"

Supposedly, Elvis bought his first guitar at the Tupelo Hardware Store. Was it a Christmas present? If Elvis was a kid now and he was offered a guitar or a Sega Genesis, which one would he choose?

I can tell you this: Route 78, which was Route 34 hasn't changed all that much. Still the same, small poor towns, like Olive Branch, Byhalia, Potts Camp, Hickory Flat and New Albany come at you out of the gray, stark winter landscape. Of them all, New Albany looks like it has grown to some extent.

After about an hour and a half of cruising along, I land in Tupelo. When I pull onto Main Street, something strange happens. My rented car stalls and the tape player that the manager at the rental place said didn't work starts to play Johnny Ace's "Pledging My Love", which is one of the most haunting songs in my life. I get out of the car and start pushing it to a space along the sidewalk. Two guys come along and help me push, and a barber comes out of his shop to lend a hand. They ask me what's the trouble, and I tell them that it's a rental and it just died. They suggest a garage that I should call to get help if the car doesn't start. I thank them and we go about our business, even though it's suddenly clear to me that I don't have any business in Tupelo.

I could walk to Elvis's old house, now called Elvis Presley Place, but I head down East Main and circle the town. I'm on East Main and South Commerce when a cold wind comes across. It's the kind of wind that cuts through to the bone, makes your fingers numb, causes the roots of your hair on the back of your

Thirty-Seven: Dirt Road Blues

neck tingle, like adrenalin, like it's preparing you for danger, or at least something that's not supposed to happen.

I turn around and see a man watching me, but as soon as I turn around, he ducks into a four story brick building. And I know right away who it is. I walk quickly toward the doorway where Elvis ducked into. I laugh. Here I've been hanging out in Memphis, waiting for Elvis to call me at the Peabody, and meanwhile he's hiding out in Tupelo. How perfect. Who would have figured to look for him here?

I duck into the doorway where I think Elvis disappeared. It's the barbershop. The man who helped me push my car is cutting the hair of an old man. They both look up when enter. I look around. No sign of Elvis.

I say, "Hi. I thought I saw a friend of mine come in here a second ago."

"Sorry. Things are slow today," the barber says. And the old man says, "Nobody here but us chickens. Right, Hank?"

"Well," I say, "sorry to bother you. And thanks for the push."

The barber says, "No bother. Any time," and he waves goodbye with a black comb and silver scissors in his right hand.

Now what do I do? I decide to walk around town for awhile before finding some diner with a lot of calendars to have lunch. You know the rules to eating on the road. Never eat at a place called Mom's, never stop at a place with a sign that reads "Truckers welcome," because truckers don't need a sign on the roof to tell them where the good eats are; never stop at a place that's sold more than a million of anything, because they don't cook food, they process it; never stop at a place with a sign on the door that says, "Shirt and Shoes Required." Would it okay if I walked in without pants?

Always eat where there are lots of trucks outside, or the smoke from the ventilator smells good, not like old grease; go where old cars are parked in front because poor people always know where to find good, cheap food. Make sure they have lots of business cards taped to the register and lots of calendars hanging on the walls, preferable none from funeral homes.

Now, before I eat, here's the anwer to Pop Quiz Number Eight. Obviously, the answer is two, Amos Jacobs. When things were going wrong for Amos, he said the following prayer to Saint Jude:

The Saint of the Impossible
May the most sacred heart of
Jesus Be Praised, Honored, Loved
and Glorified, now and forever,
more adorned. St. Jude, worker
of Miracles, helper of the hopeless,
pray for me that my prayers will
by answered, and I will build a
shrine to you.

Amos Jacobs said this prayer nine times a day, every day of his life, after asking Saint Jude for guidance and deliverance. Amos Jacobs prayed to become famous, and he did. No, this isn't Famous Amos. Amos Jacobs, with the huge nose, average singing voice and moderate comedic talent changed his name to Danny Thomas. Did he make movies? Yes, eight. His best role was as Gus Kahn in "I'll See You In My Dreams." Did he record? Yes. One of the ways Danny Thomas raised money to build St. Jude's Children's Hospital was to record songs in Arabic (Thomas was Lebanese) and sell them for a dollar. Some of these recordings now fetch several hundred dollars on the vintage record market. Was he a tv star? Sure. "Make Room For Daddy." He also went on to produce "The Andy Griffith Show," "The Dick Van Dyke Show." among others.

Eventually, he fulfilled his promise by building the Saint Jude's Children's Hospital, in Memphis. And that hospital has saved more kids' lives than any other single institution in the world. Does he deserve a boulevard named after him? Yes. More than Elvis? Yes! All Elvis brought to Memphis was money. All Danny Thomas brought to Memphis was hope and a real chance for children diagnosed with cancer to live.

Now, to find a good place to eat.

Thirty-Eight: The Sanctified Shot-Gun In A One Room Sharecropper's House

On the grill the short order cook is killing a couple of hamburgers until they're crisp and almost too hard to eat. He turns away from the grill, a half smoked cigarette dangling between his tight lips. He looks at me glaringly, like leprosy is crawling over me or that maybe I was born under a bad sign. He grumbles at me asking what I want. I scan the greasy plastic covered menu and settle on a rib sandwich and coffee. You ever notice how people in a small town can spot an outsider in a second, then treat him like he's got some disease that is highly contagious? Same thing here. I watch the cook put my sandwich together to make sure he doesn't pull a Jesse Jackson. In his autobiography, the Reverend Jackson says that when he worked in a diner he used to spit on the food of white people. I eat the rib sandwich. It's delicious, but I don't enjoy it. I don't even finish my coffee. I toss a sawbuck on the counter just to let the cook know that I'm not just some bum traveling through. I've got money to burn. Glare at me, you son of a bitch. I throw back one of my own mean-eyed stares and head outside.

I go back to my rented car, certain that it's gotten over its emotional shutdown. I decide to drive over to Elvis's childhood house. It's been a good twenty years since I've come through here. The place was in ruin then. When I get to Elvis's old house, it's obvious that someone in Tupelo has recognized the value of the old house as a major tourist attraction. Everything is painted white. Planted some bushes in front of the house. Put a shrine behind the house where the outhouse used to be so people can pray for the lost soul of Elvis. Everything clean, sanitized and sanctified, like Vernon, Elvis, and no one in the Presley family, except maybe Gladys, ever was.

It's amazing what we do to old buildings and old idols. We freeze them in time, purified of all crimes and demons. The inside of the house is as beautiful as you can make a make-shift Depression-built shot gun house. If you stand still in what was the living room, you can't imagine the maroon horse-hair filled used couch Vernon brought back from the dump. You can't feel the heat of the small oil stove that was used to heat the fron of the house. You can't imagine the black Glenwood cast iron stove Gladys cooked on, a kettle of water constantly heating on one of the two back burners, or the silver painted copper hot water heater that had to be lit manually whenever someone in the family wanted hot water for a bath. There is no sign of the old linoleum, no sign of the newspapers that were stuffed in the northeast ceiling where the roof leaked.

Everything is so clean, so new, the place has been robbed of its spirit, as though poverty is something we have to hide, bury the sins of the father, in this case, Vernon, raw, barely literate, unskilled, and willing to steal for his family. Some might see that as a character flaw, but I see that as a strength. It takes real courage to steal for your family, especially when you know to consequences and are willing to pay the price. Most people pass over the importance of Vernon. Dismiss him as a no count thief and forger. I admire him. He was a great father, given the tools he had and the time and place in Tupelo, Mississippi in the Great Depression. He saw himself, as husband and father, as the provider, and Vernon provided. He suffered on his own cross. An infant child dying, time in prison, menial, meaningless jobs. Even when Vernon would eventually fly with Elvis on one of his private jets, Vernon was still the nearly illiterate, living in mental poverty, always out of place and constantly fearing the worst: the

Thirty-Eight: The Sanctified Shot-Gun

lights going out because of an unpaid bill, the long walk home to face Gladys and Elvis and tell them he had been fired again, and at night, unable to sleep because of his constant fear of someone with a badge knocking on his door to take him away. God bless the soul and spirit of Vernon Presley. May we each me as loving and caring as he was.

I don't hang around the Presley house for very long. If Elvis wants to see me, he knows where to find me, but I'm not going to play cat and mouse with him in Tupelo. It's too damned cold. Besides, if I step on it, I can get back to the Peabody in time to hear Bill Cinton's address to the people on the economy. Yesterday he said everyone will have to make a sacrifice. Today his mouthpieces say what President Bill meant was that we'll all have to contribute, not sacrifice, to reduce the national debt. Well, that's different. I might not be willing to sacrifice, yes, of course I'd be willing to contribute.

I'm overcome by this feeling that I can't get out of Mississippi. I first came down here in the early Sixties. James Meredith got shot trying to go to Old Miss. This is where Medgar Evers was killed. We know they found three bodies of Civil Rights Workers, but how many didn't they find?

I would like to speed, but I know that if I do I'll get stopped, so I push the limit but don't exceed it. I must be getting old.

About fifty miles from the Mississippi-Tennessee border, I get stuck behind a Greyhound bus. I try to pass the bus, but every time I try the driver swerves the bus in front of me. Then driver slows down to about twenty miles and hour, even though the speed limit is 55. It's getting dark and storm clouds are gathering behind me in the southeastern sky, where the really bad storms come from. I just don't like what's going on. Usually there's a lot of traffic on 78 between five and six o'clock in the evening, but now there's nothing. I begin to wonder what the short order cook at the dive in Tupelo put in my coffee, because the sky is turning purple.

Any minute I expect my rental car to stall, but it doesn't. You know, there is a lot to spells and voodoo. Somebody could put a fix on you, a real mean *gris-gris,* and you wouldn't even know it, except everything you do seems to go wrong. Sticks and bricks rain down on your house for no reason. You might find a fire in your mail box or things in your house begin to disappear. You want to blame someone, but it's all spirit work. And it works the other way, too. I have seen people at the end of a hopeless terminal illness, go to a Voodooienne and given cures, such as drinking rooster blood, burning blue candles, or wearing metal pieces cut in the shapes of special totems, or bathing in waters filled with the essence of honeysuckle and verbena and pine needle oil. And some of these people rise from their beds cured. It depends on how much you believe. Just like the Catholic Church with its rituals and mystery. To get you through the dark waters you have to have Jesus as your Captain and the Holy Ghost on the tiller.

I've seen Voodoo and mind over matter work on and for other people, but it never worked on me. Before now, that is. But that's how I feel. Something strange is upon me, overtaking me, traveling through time to eternity, into a strange landscape. I feel like I'm in the bottom half of a double boiler. I know the heat's on, but I don't know what's cooking.

I try to pass the Greyhound again, but the driver speeds up. I speed up, too, but he tries to cut me off. Wouldn't you know it, he doesn't have one of those "Tell me if you like my driving" signs with an 800 number stuck to the back of his bus.

I decide to fall back. Let him think I've gotten tired of his little game. But when I slow down, so does the bus. I try to pass again, and the bus speeds up. I fall back again, and the bus slows down. This is war and the sign of the judgment. I turn my headlights off, floor it, and pass that maniac on the right side of the bus before he knows what's happening. He tries to catch up, but he's got too much weight to haul. I turn back and think about flipping him the bird, but when I look up I can see the driver. He's laughing. He's pointing and laughing at me. And Jesus, Mary, and Joseph,

Thirty-Eight: The Sanctified Shot-Gun

the driver looks just like Robert Johnson, skull head pulled tight over brown skin, wide eyes sunk deep in their sockets, cigarette dangling from his taut, leathery lips and he's laughing, laughing as though he knows I might have gotten away now but he will have the last laugh. I just keep driving while the winds come up and rain begins to pelt my windshield with a rock hard steady beat. I watch the headlights of the bus get smaller in my rear view mirror and then disappear and for some unknown reason I think about Jesus, that he died for our sins and was risen and seated at the right hand of God. But that's all right for him. I, for one, have spent my life looking for an original sin, only to find out that all the ones I've tried have been done before.

I'm sure it's something I ate or drank, because I know I'm seeing more than what's there like the purple sky and the faces of Robert E. Lee and Walt Whitman in the swirling, dark storm clouds. I keep that accelerator to the floor, speeding ticket or no, and I don't feel safe until I cross into Tennessee and see the lights of Memphis on the horizon.

I get back to the Peabody, check for mail and messages. One phone call, but no message. The person will try to reach me later. It's dinner time, but I have no desire to eat. I go into the lounge and have a couple of stiff ones, watch part of a basketball game on ESPN, which is something I never do. But sports never change. The players get bigger and less graceful. Now it takes five steps to be called for traveling instead of three. When did basketball become a contact sport? No blood, no foul. There's one player who's really good. Can rebound, play D, pass, and shoot from outside, named Scott Burrell. Senior year in college. Next year he'll be a millionaire. I hoist a glass to him, wish him well in this world of mystery and surprise.

At half-time, I head to my room, take a shower, turn on the tube. I've missed Clinton's budget report. I turn to Sherlock Holmes, on A & E. It's "The Six Napoleons," a good story, but I'm asleep, dead to the world, before Holmes can intuit the solution.

Thirty-Nine: Sweet Home Arizona

They're burying Baby Doe this morning in Memphis. Baby Doe was found ten days ago, a few hours old, frozen to death. He's in a small, wooden casket painted white. Someone's placed a small, white stuffed rabbit alongside the infant's body. What a planet. We live at a time when there are a dozen ways you can prevent getting pregnant. If you get pregnant, you can get an abortion legally in most places. If you don't want to get an abortion, there are a thousand places that will take care of your sweet angel baby. There is just no reason to dump a newborn infant in the snow. I'd like to find that bitch myself. In the words of Robert Johnson, "I'm gonna upset your backbone, put your kidneys to sleep. I'll break away your liver and dare your heart to beat." *

Times are cold in Memphis. I call the Pioneer Hotel in Tucson, and make my reservation. Ah, beautiful Tucson. Overgrown cattle town. Probably 75 degrees during the day. I need a recharge. My pilot light is out. Need to go out into the desert. Get some trail dust in my lungs. I have had my fill of grey days. Memphis is okay, but maybe I'll come back in the spring when the sun is out more.

I call the desk to get my bill together. Mr. Tutwiler is sorry to see me go, but I assure him that I'll be back to visit my money. He laughs and tells me that I must be joking. I lie and tell him I am. I get dressed and head to Beale Street one last time.

*copyright 1990, King of Spades Music.

Urban renewal had taken almost everything wonderful from Beale Street. The old, funky joints, the Black hotels, those little

Thirty-Nine: Sweet Home Arizona

drug stores where you could buy Rooster Pills, Rythm Oil, Dixie Peach, and buy B.B. King LP's on Kent Records for $1.98. That's all gone. Then there was Lansky's, a dollar down and a dollar a week. What next? Next thing they'll be urban renewing will be us. They'll put out postage stamps honoring Barry Manilow or Barbra Streisand, Tony Orlando & Dawn. Let the statue of W. C. Handy rot and erect one to honor Don King, personifier of the American dream and hustler extra modum.

One thing that I wanted to do while I was here but didn't was to go to Al Green's church. In the world there is the Catholic Church, the Congregational Church, the Church of the Rock, St. Stephen's Church, and the Cathedral in the Pines. But in Memphis, we got Al Green's Church. Al Green goes back in Memphis history. He started out on Hi Records, Bill Black's label, with a hit called "Tired of Being Alone," back in 1971.

He had a bunch of hits after that, including "Let's Stay Together" and "Look at What You've Done For Me." Notice the lack of self pity, or self-effacing victimization that would have occurred if he changed "for" to "to", which was a refreshing break from the usual Otis Redding, Sam Cooke, Solomon Burke soul lyrics where love is an evil force. You know, "If Loving You Is Wrong, I Don't Want To Be Right."

Somewhere along the way, Al Green recognized that his music had run its course. Maybe it was when a woman who claimed she loved him poured a pot of boiling grits over him, then killed herself. Or maybe he saw that the music business for the racket it is. He got out and into the ministry. Not like Little Richard did, when a bolt of lightning struck the plane he was on during turbulent weather, flying on tour to Australia. Little Richard got down on the floor of that plane and said, "Jesus, Jeezus, Jeez us please, if you get me out of this, I'll give up rock and roll, I'll give up the devil's music for the sweet and everlasting harmonies of that Heavenly chorus." Well, Little Richard survived, dabbled in the church for awhile, then realized that there was no money in preaching, so he hit the road again, only to be on another plane, during another storm, on his knees, praying to the great deliverer, and I don't mean Nolan Ryan. Well, Little Richard took up preaching again, but rock and roll called and he took to the road, going no where unless it had a train.

Al Green never looked back. And if there is a spiritual center in Memphis, if after all its transgressions, Memphis hasn't been abandoned, awashed in its sins, then Al Green's Church is that place. If you want bad taste, mythology, and examples on how not to live, go to Graceland. If it's sanctificatied you want to be, then you know where you must go. But please, if you're going to dress like a tourist and gawk like the cracker you can't help your sorry ass self from being, go to Graceland.

Forty: The Final Exam

Question One. It's difficult to believe that anyone ever outsold a recording by Elvis, but it did happen. Which combination of musicians outsold Elvis? Was it:
    a. Jim Stafford, Johnny Cash, Billy Joe Dupree and Carl Perkins.
    b. Roy Orbison, Johnny Cash, Jerry Lee Lewis, and Carl Perkins.
    c. Terry Stafford, Roseanne Cash, Johnny Paycheck, and Carl Perkins.
    d. George Jones, Merle Haggard, Waylon Jennings, and Carl Perkins.

Question Two. Elvis wanted to join which singing group?
    a. The Ronettes
    b The Drifters
    c. Jan & Dean
    d. The Holy Jesus Mountain Movers
    e. The Detroit Jewels
    f. The Blackwood Brothers
    g. The Song Fellows

Question Three. When Elvis was released from active duty, in 1960, his first appearance was on a tv show emceed by:
    a. Tennessee Ernie Ford
    b. Ed Sullivan
    c. Steve Allen
    d. Frank Sinatra
    e. Milton Berle

Question Four. Elvis paid to have two songs cut at Memphis Recording Service. Elvis was on the right track because both songs became million sellers for other artists by the end of the decade. Who were the artists and what were the songs' titles?
    a. Blueberry Hill by Antoine Domino
    b. One Night by Smiley Lewis
    c. My Happiness by Connie Francis
    d. Harbor Lights by The Platters
    e. Big Boss Man by Jimmy Reed
    f. Blue Suede Shoes by Carl Perkins

Question Five. In 1955 Elvis auditioned for and was turned down by:
    a. Ted Mack's Original Amateur Hour
    b. The Jackie Gleason Show
    c. Colgate Variety Hour
    d. Arthur Godfrey's Talent Scouts

Question Six. Elvis never appeared on which of the following tv shows?
    a. Tommy and Jimmy Dorsey's Stage Show
    b. The Roy Orbison Show
    c. American Bandstand
    d. Milton Berle's Texaco Star Theater
    e. Shindig

Question Seven. Elvis's first movie was supposed to be:
    a. The Rainmaker with Burt Lancaster
    b. Giant with James Dean
    c. Blackboard Jungle with Glenn Ford
    d. Operation Madball with Ernie Kovacs
    e. Miracle in the Rain with Van Johnson

Question Eight. The least price paid for a mint Sun Recording of "That's All Right" with a red "DJ Copy" stamped on the label. Was it"
  a. $2,200
  b. $600
  c. $1,250
  d. 7 cents
  e. $175

Okay, let's see how you did. Always the same hands. Question one. The correct answer is b. Johnny Cash's version of "I Forgot to Remember to Forget", Carl Perkin's version of "Blue Suede Shoes", and Roy Orbison's and Jerry Lee Lewis's versions of "Mean Woman Blues" each outsold Elvis's versions of the same songs. Oddly enough, Perkins, Lewis, Cash and Orbison were all alumni of Sun Records, Elvis' first recording label.

Question Two. I'm not going to say that Elvis didn't want to join the Ronettes (who wouldn't), but he never stated so publicly. I know he didn't want to join The Holy Jesus Mountain Movers, because they don't exist. The brand name of my antique gas stove is Detroit Jewels. Every time I look at the grey letters of the white porcelain I think, "What a great name for a singing group." Even though Elvis admired The Blackwood Brothers, it is a subsidiary of the Blackwood Brothers, namely, The Song Fellows, that Elvis had hope to join back in 1954-55. So, the answer to Question two is g.

Question Three. The correct answer is d, Frank Sinatra. You could see it going down from there. Of course, Elvis could have appeared on The Tennessee Ernie Ford Show, that was on the same time as the Elvis-Sinatra special. If you did watch Ernie Ford that night, you would have seen Johnny Cash and the Tennessee Three.

Question Four. The two songs that Elvis recorded on his own were c and d, "My Happiness" and "Harbor Lights", each millions sellers for Connie Francis and the Platters respectively in the late Fifties.

Question Five. Elvis auditioned for and was turned down by d, Arthur Godfrey's Talent Scouts. On the other hand, Lenny Bruce, Wally Cox, Tony Bennett and Mr. Excitement, Pat Boone, were among the stars discovered on Arthur Godfrey's Talent Scouts a weekly half hour show seen on CBS on Monday nights in the mid-1950's.

Question Six. Elvis never appeared on Dick Clark's American Bandstand. We're not sure that this was due to good taste or happenstance. Elvis never appeared on Shindig either. So, the correct answers are c and e. Elvis debuted on Tommy and Jimmy Dorsey Stage Show, and he appeared on Roy Orbison's local tv show, in 1955, sponsored by Pioneer furniture, out of Odessa, Texas. Kinescope, anyone?

Question Seven. Elvis's first role was supposed to be opposite Burt Lancaster, in "The Rainmaker". The answer is a.

Question Eight is: what is the best price anyone has paid for a mint recording of "That's All Right" ? The answer is d, seven cents. My friend John Pinkney and I learned that an old record collector had died and his wife donated his records to Goodwill, Inc. on Grand Avenue, in New Haven, Connecticut. John and I got there, but there were a number of vinyl junkies ahead of us. There were 10,000s of records in rows across eight tables that were about twenty feet long. The 45's were placed in alphabetical order. John, who looks a lot like Elvis, headed for the "P's". A collector was there ahead of him. The collector said, "If you're looking for Elvis, forget it. I got 'em all," and he held up his right hand, displaying a bunch of RCA labels.

What the hell, John and I start looking through the bin anyway. In a few minutes, John pulls out a DJ copy of "That's All Right" on Sun Records. John pulls out a few other records because he doesn't want to go to the cashier with just the Sun Record showing. John asks the Goodwill cashier how much the records are. He bought fifteen. She says, "Give me a dollar, including tax. Is that all right?"

All right? I guess it was all right. Think how many boxes you've looked through, hoping to find gold.

Forty: The Final Exam

Each question is worth eight divided into one hundred. As always, neatness, straight margins and originality of thought count. At least, that's what they used to tell me in school. Some of my wrong answers were really original, but they never counted.

Forty-One: The Phone Call

It's two a.m. and I'm up in room 1238 at the Peabody. Some Thelonious Monk Blue Note sides are playing on my Sony Walkperson CD player. Tomorrow at this time I'll have spent the day in the sun in Madera Canyon, just north of Tucson. There are so many people angry with me in Tucson, I don't know who to call and piss off first.

Some of my favorite years were spent in Tucson. Did I ever tell you about the time I lived with Kerouac's niece? That was a long time ago, but sometimes at night I swear I hear her voice. As Mississippi Fred McDowell used to say, "No matter how much you got, time ain't much."

I'm listening to an alternate take of "Suburban Eyes" through the headphones, and I almost don't hear the telephone. Two a.m. I pick it up and say hello. I should have known. A cheery Elvis is on the other end. "Hi," he says, then laughs. "Well," I ask, "what the hell was that all about?"

"I can't tell you. I'm leaving for Germany. I want you to promise me one thing."

"Sure," I tell him.

"I can't explain, but forget about writing that book. Or at least wait until The Colonel and Sam Phillip are gone."

"Gone for real. or gone like you."

"Look," he says, "who's going to believe it anyway? Just forget it."

"What happened last month? Who were those guys?"

"Trust me. I can't tell anyone anything right now."

Forty-One: The Phone Call

"You say you're going to Germany. Does that mean you're going to Peoria?"

"Yeah," Elvis says, "something like that. But I'll be back. You're on the list. I'll let you know."

"Well, if it's really important to you that I don't put this book together, I'll start sending it around tomorrow.."

"You serious?"

"You're right. Who's going to believe it? It's a good thing I'm taping this conversation."

"One, I know you're not taping this. And two, do you have any idea how many tapes of phone conversations of me there are out there, and *nobody* believes them? That's how it is. Everyone wants to believe but they're afraid. Everyone wants to see God, but when someone says they've seen Elvis, they lock him up. Hey, Duke, I've talked too long. Thanks for the good times and hiding me out. I knew you were leaving Memphis tonight. Sorry I couldn't talk to you yesterday in Tupelo. But I wanted to say goodbye. When I get back I'll let you know."

Elvis hangs up. Thelonious is playing "Well, You Needn't". I place the phone back on its cradle and go back to packing. Elvis in Germany. It is possible, but not likely. Too much trouble using a passport and passing customs. My guess is that he will stay in the south, at least until the spring. He has a few friends he can trust in Arkansas. He has a daughter there who is in college majoring in Literature. And that reminds me. I started telling you about Tucson. Kerouac's niece. Karen. Beautiful eyes. That long auburn hair. She got arrested in Tasco, Mexico for possession and I never heard from her again. And there was another woman. Jane. She was into The Who, Meher Baba, and agronomy at the University of Arizona. Meher Baba, who had taken a vow of silence, used to hand out small business-sized cards with his beautiful, bearded face on them, with the words: "Don't worry, be happy," decades before Bobby McFerrin came along.

God, I remember when Rainbow, the son of the Yaqui chief, was staying with me on Herbert Avenue, because his father wanted

Rainbow to learn how life was off the reservation. Rainbow and I had just dropped acid when Jane came by with some coke and a rolled up hundred dollar bill. Jane said, "You get higher when you use a humdred dollar bill." Jane, Rainbow and I went into Sabino Canyon, south of Tucson. When we got there we built a fire because night was coming on and it had gotten cold. I was staring at the flames, and they were staring back. They looked like dancing hydras. Jane was saying something, but I couldn't answer. She seemed miles away. Rainbow was playing a harmonica, or maybe it was the wind blowing through the rocks and ledges in Sabino Canyon

When I looked up from the flames, I was in Gallop, New Mexico, at the house of Frank Takes Gun, the spiritual leader of the Native American Church. I asked Frank how I got there. Frank Takes Gun said he didn't know. He had been eating some peyote an hour earlier and until I spoke, he thought that I was just another one of his visions. We just looked at each other in the shadowy sanctuary of the Native American Church and shrugged our shoulders, as if to say, "What do I know?" From there I went to Taos and met this artist who had a cabin. She lived alone with her son. She said if you need a place to write, I've got one. But, as they say in Como, Mississippi, that's a whole 'nother story.

About the Author

Franz Douskey has published in hundreds of magazines, including *Rolling Stone, The New Yorker, Down East, Las Vegas Life, The Nation, Yankee, Cavalier* and *Center*. He was nominated for a Pulitzer Prize in 2011 for his book *West of Midnight*. In 2012, Douskey published *Sinatra and Me: The Very Good Years*, co-written with Tony Consiglio. His more than 100 recent appearances include the Judith Regan Show on Sirius Radio, Jim Bohannan, Imus In The Morning (six repeats), and a signing at Mohegan Sun Casino in Connecticut.

Made in the USA
Lexington, KY
10 March 2014